Books by L.A. Kennedy

The Genesys Project

Immortal Amour
Dark Amour

I0545941

Dark Amour

ISBN # 978-1-78651-352-6

Cover Art by Posh Gosh ©Copyright 2016

Interior text design by Claire Siemaszkiewicz

Totally Bound Publishing

Published in 2016 by Totally Bound Publishing, Newland House, The Point, Weaver Road, Lincoln, LN6 3QN, United Kingdom.

Totally Bound Publishing is a subsidiary of Totally Entwined Group Limited.

The Genesys Project

DARK AMOUR

L.A. KENNEDY

Dedication

Dedicated to my mother... As the saying goes, you walked uphill, both ways, in hip-deep snow, with bags for shoes. That was your journey to make sure I succeeded and I know you'd have dug through hell with your bare hands and crawled through glass for me.

Thank you with so much love for being there to remove my self-doubt, and for each time you said, "You can be anything in life. I believe in you." I can never repay you for all you have done. Thank you for encouraging my dreams and for always being there when I stumbled.

And for Van... To the academic, the brain, the Google master, the friend, the snack maker and the lover in you, thank you. For each time you looked up with a smile when I ranted about my characters, I appreciate those moments. Thank you for understanding I had to work on my last chapter and couldn't dig myself out from behind my new creation. Thank you for making this as important to you as it is to me. While you have been along for my ride, I thank you for inviting me to be along for yours. It's been one hell of a ride!

P.S. Don't touch the chocolates on the fridge, I've "literally" staked claim!

Acknowledgments

With immense gratitude to Jamie Rose, my editor, slash coach, slash cheerleader. I could go on for hours here. You wear many hats with me. I can't say enough about how amazing you are. I am blessed to have someone like you in my corner. Thank you for always having the time to answer my questions and guide me toward my dream.

A huge thank you to the rest of the team at TEG. You all blow me away. Emmy, your creativity is far more than I could have hoped for. I'd like to thank each and every one of you, but there are so many to list. I feel blessed to be able to say there are so many people on board with me. Thank you.

And a special thank you to my readers, my writer friends, and my family—both blood related and chosen. None of this would be possible without your support and encouragement. From the bottom of my heart, thank you.

Chapter One

Zylan-Nefarious Bloodletting must die.

Zylan—Zy to his friends—was born cursed and heir to the throne of Sola-Nosfer, a ruling Vampyre hamlet, the settlement of the upper crust of their society. He was the blood descendant of Rhival-Enmity Bloodletting and Vestal Virgyn Zylamon-Vhenom Bloodletting. They were the ruling king and queen for almost six hundred years.

Upon his birth, he was promised to the hand of Amity-Rhuin Blooddawn at the age of thirty. Amity was the blood descendant of Vhenom-Ash Blooddawn, High Councilman, and daughter of Ayla-Dhemise Blooddawn, Vestal Virgyn.

With his thirtieth birthday upon him, Zy needed to die his first death. It was law. It was to be celebrated with the Reaping. His people would come from around the world to watch him take his last breath as a Day Walkyr, his first life harvested for the betterment of his people and the continuation of his bloodline. Basically, he'd be held down and his throat slashed, while the uppity-ups drank wine and laughed full-bellied, pretentious laughs, lifting their glasses, spilling their wine, all in the name of some tradition that most of them couldn't remember why they even celebrated. There would be free booze, free food and free access to royalty. That was all that mattered to them. Zy grimaced at the idea. *Useless, each and every one of them.*

Zy had left Sola-Nosfer at the age of twenty. He was granted ten years, less one day, to explore the outside world. Due to his childhood training in the Vampyres' version of *The Art of War*, the Netherworld had accepted him right away. He'd been put into the field within months, and he'd finally landed undercover with Cael and Riam. To him, it was the best thing that could have ever happened to him. With Cael and Riam, Zy finally felt at home, with a family who truly cared. Unfortunately for him, it wasn't as long-lasting as he would have hoped. He knew the drill. *You can't run from fate.*

Day Walkyrs were called home the day before they turned thirty in preparation for the first death. *Nothing says 'welcome home' like having your throat slashed.*

To not return meant being banished from society for the rest of the Vampyre's days and having a black smear placed upon that family name. Zylan would've been happy with being banished. But, in his case, he would have been hunted. It was absolute law for him to return to marry his promised one. The duty flowed through his veins, as it had done for his parents and their parents. Some traditions weren't easily dismissed — not for him and not in his family.

Sitting in the corner of his bedroom on the floor, he held his invitation to the Reaping, his name listed as the one to be celebrated. In exactly three months, a blade would be dragged across his throat, his blood flowing into solid gold bowls and fed to the high born and patrician of his society. They'd toast his death with the very blood that kept his heart beating.

He'd met Amity-Rhuin Blooddawn once, if he could call it that. The day he was leaving Sola-Nosfer, she'd been there. He hadn't stopped to talk to her, and he hadn't bothered looking in her direction. He hadn't wanted to marry her then, and those feelings hadn't changed with time. With a taste of the outside world, he hated the idea more now than ever. How could he go back? How could he marry someone he didn't love? How could he abandon his fellow Slayers?

With the invitation came a photo of Amity. He stared at the photo, finding himself glaring. He almost hated her in all her beauty and perfection. She was as beautiful as she should have been for the son of a king and queen. He knew her manners would be impeccable, and she would give appreciation for any verbal assault her husband would offer her. And she'd do it with a smile and not a tear in sight. She'd likely not know what the word 'no' was, as she was raised to be agreeable and free of complaint. She would be nothing like the spitfire and hellish women found in the clubs around Van City. Here they dressed in stilettos, wore an inch of makeup and had an attitude. The only silver lining? Amity wouldn't be coked out of her skull or need to be shoulder-packed home, lost to drunken oblivion. In all honesty, Zy would sooner foot the bill for a coked-out bitch.

For Amity to fail was to sign her death certificate. She would be entombed with a small amount of food and water then left to die, unless the Orygin decided to save her, which he wouldn't. He never did. It was his society's way of putting the responsibility of her death onto someone else, someone their traditions said was untouchable, the Orygin. Amity would be dressed it up in a pretty dress and the act would be called something other than what it truly was — murder. *Yep, these are my people, lost to their ignorant ways.*

Amity would be like the rest of those promised to the royal born. She'd kowtow to her husband and thank him for any cruelties he saw fit to bestow upon her delicate body. Her breeding was exact. There would be no flaws. She'd come from a long line of Vestal Virgyns, and she would produce all female children to take their places within the Vestal Virgyn ranks, save one or two male children to carry on the family name. For every three females, a male child would be born. Most Vestal Virgyns did not produce more than eight children, if they weren't killed by their husbands beforehand. But that didn't matter. Zy didn't want a single one with her, let alone eight. Eight little reminders of what he could have had, but he'd had to settle for.

Her skin was china doll white and flawless, and she had ice-blue eyes and white-blonde hair in waves to her hips. She had an ample bosom, small waist, long legs, and she was hairless everywhere but her head. The photo left nothing to the imagination. She stood nude, not being allowed to cover her body in any way. *It is our way.* She belonged to Zy, and she could hide nothing from him. It was more of an ownership than anything else. His people put more care into trading livestock than marriage.

Blood of my blood, blood of your blood, cemented an eight-hundred-year-old truce. Zylan's father's father had conquered the neighboring lands, and the practice remained. The neighboring council members now presided over one council. Zylan was to marry the most influential of them all, the daughter of the High Councilman.

He wished he was like Cael, the Aegys of the Slayers — their protector, leader and guardian of the newbies. Cael, of a lost family line, was free. Cael was adopted after damn near dying at the hands of his abusive parents. He'd been thrown away, left for dead. He was Vampyre, without any ties to the godforsaken society. *Lucky him.*

Zy opened the invitation, oddly careful not to rip the thick-papered envelope. The whitest of white — only the purest for his mother, a once-was Vestal Virgyn. Everything was perfect, as always. She didn't sleep unless it was perfect. Perfect breeding wasn't something a Vestal Virgyn outgrew.

Zylan pulled the blood-red card from the thick envelope, running his fingers over the embossed white lettering. He knew his mother had spent months, if not years, designing this card perfectly. It was who she was.

The Reaping
The Reaping Celebration of Prince Zylan-Nefarious Bloodletting
King Rhival-Enmity Bloodletting
and
Queen Zylamon-Vhenom Bloodletting
are proud to announce the Reaping of their son,
Prince Zylan-Nefarious Bloodletting
Date of birthing celebrated October nine in the year nineteen hundred and eighty-six.
Date of rebirthing to be celebrated on October nine in the year

two thousand and sixteen.

Your presence is requested at midnight. We invite you to celebrate this new beginning.

Zylan cringed. He had fewer than ninety days until he'd drag his sorry ass back to his mother and father, back to a world he wanted nothing to do with. If he stayed with the Slayers, the king and queen—Ma and Pa—would kill him to remove the disgrace he would bring to his family. They would also kill everyone who harbored him. If he returned to Sola-Nosfer, he'd be forced to marry Amity, and he'd be forever stuck in a loveless marriage with a woman he knew he'd grow to hate even more. Amity wasn't who Zylan wanted, and he'd hate her for it.

Sola-Nosfer wasn't a bad place. It was what it represented that Zylan didn't like. He pulled his cell phone from his pocket, making a call he should have made nineteen years ago.

"Mother," Zylan whispered.

"Zylan, it has been too long." Her voice was void of emotion. His mother wasn't created to allow emotion. She was created for one thing, birthing more royals and bowing when her mate, Zylan's father, entered the room.

But Zy knew her. He knew her heart had skipped a beat with excitement to hear from her son. When he was a child and no one was looking, his mother would smile or cry or groan in frustration. She was—and always would be—more than her birth to Zylan.

"I've received the card," Zylan spoke, his bones vibrating with the need to scream that he didn't want to come back. He wanted to rant and rave, throw down the gauntlet, but he knew it was pointless.

"We look forward to your return. We all do. Your younger brother will return for the night. He, like you, has been gone for many years."

Zylan sighed, trying to stifle it to keep his mother from hearing the sadness in his exhalation. Zylan had one younger brother, who was out exploring the world, and six older sisters, all Vestal Virgyns. He didn't know who to pity more, the younger brother who would be yanked back, forced to give up everything and everyone – including any children he may have been foolish enough to produce out in the free world – or his sisters, who would be forced to marry into the highest of society, likely away from the family and home they knew, into loveless marriages.

"You do not want to return, son of mine?" she asked in a monotone voice. Zylan knew his mother already had the answer. She was never the fool.

"No, I do not." His answer was straight and to the point.

"You must. It is your duty. Amity is in waiting. She is to complete the Reaping the night before yours. She has committed her life to serving you."

Zylan closed his eyes, praying he'd wake up and be someone else to find that this was all just one long fucking nightmare.

"I want to see her, here, before the Reaping. I want to know who I'm being forced to marry and produce heirs and more virgins with because of this barbaric and pointless tradition."

His mother let out a long, frustrated sigh. "Son, you insult me with your words, for I once was a Vestal Virgyn. There is great honor in that role. We bring forth our most noble, our warriors, our most honorable. If not for me, you would not be here to offer such insults."

Cursing himself, he apologized. "I'm not prepared for this, Mother. I'm sorry. You've done nothing wrong. You've only ever done right by me. It's just difficult to give up my life."

"I will send Amity to you at once. I believe you may be correct. Had I known your father and had been given time to love him, perhaps life would have been easier for both of us. It took many years for us to love each other. I wish you not to have that pain or suffering."

"Pain and suffering... Isn't that what we're about? You could've fooled me." He didn't bother keeping his anger out of his comment.

After a long pause, his mother spoke again. She was almost an expert in governing her emotions, but Zylan could hear the sadness in the silence.

"My heart aches for you, my son. I will send the pure Vestal Virgyn to you at once. Use caution with her. She is not of your world. She has spent time there, learning the ways you would return home with, but she is not accustomed to them all. Please be of kindness."

"Thank you, Mother," Zylan replied.

They both hung up. No one spoke words of love in his family home. Love was weakness. It was a tool to be used against opponents. Zy remembered what his father had said about love. *'You do not love, you do not mourn and you are not tender or kind or forgiving. You are ruthless. To be a ruler, you have to be willing to kill your own children with your bare hands as they sleep in their cribs.'*

Zylan felt cursed. He would not be one of the privileged. He would not get to live out his life with the one he loved. And Zylan did love someone, but her name wasn't Amity.

He pressed the back of his head into the wall he was leaning against. He had to go to Cael and inform him of what was happening with Amity and her impending arrival, but he was currently avoiding Cael.

Earlier in the evening, Cael had called a team meeting of the Slayers. It had gone as well as removing a spider with a fire bomb. For the first time in his career with Cael, when Cael pushed, Zylan had pushed back with force. It played over and over in his mind now, since the moment he'd drawn that line in the sand.

"God damn it, Cael. We don't need her!" Zylan had yelled, leaning across the long wooden table. He'd felt the angry heat in his cheeks. He'd known his face had to have been bright red, and his eyes had been almost surely about to pop out of their sockets.

Cael had paced. He did this when he was nervous about something. And after he'd opened his mouth, everyone had known why he was pacing. Cael had been asking Zylan to bring in his Fyrvor.

He'd stood firm against Cael, the makeshift leader of the Slayers. His body had been vibrating, the table legs tapping the floor from the fury flowing out of his hands. Cael wasn't one to back down. Zylan knew this, but he wasn't backing down either, not when it came to his Fyrvor. No one backed down when it came to their only reason for breathing.

The Slayers had stood shoulder to shoulder in the main hall. A long table ran twenty feet in length, down the middle of the room. There had been fourteen of them left, seven on each side—Cael on one side and Zylan on the other. After four months, they had been down a few, lost to the war against the Proletaryans and the Order.

"We do, Zy. We need Nerissa," Cael had spoken, his voice soft, like he understood exactly how Zylan felt.

Zylan had pointed at Des, Cael's Fyrvor. "We fought to keep *her* out of this. I spent weeks, months—hell, years—trying to keep your Fyrvor away from this. I was paying rent in her fucking buildings to keep an eye on her for you. I followed her around like a bloody puppy dog, making sure she was solid, because you couldn't go out in the daylight. And now you want to pull in the one person I love?"

"She doesn't know you love her," a voice had interrupted them both. Riam, with no last name, put his two cents in, earning a glare from both Cael and Zylan.

"Do you know a Kler'odient who's stronger than she is? Who can read the future? One who knows the dormant irregular gene as well as she does?" Cael had asked. "She's the only one who fits the bill, the only one who can do what we need. Are you willing to risk the entire race of irregulars for her?"

Zylan had pounded the table. His shoulders had shaken with the need to punch something, someone. "Yes! Are you happy? Yes, I'm willing to risk the world for her. Aren't you willing to do the same for Des?"

Des had stepped forward, shaking her head. "No. He

damn well isn't, and he shouldn't be. I wouldn't risk you all for him. I wouldn't risk the citizens who are counting on us for him. I'd want to, but I wouldn't. I'd want to watch the world burn to the ground for him, but I wouldn't. That isn't what love is. That's infatuation. That's ownership. Cael would kill for me. He'd kill one of you to protect me. He'd die for me, but he wouldn't sentence the rest of you to the same fate. He, like me, wouldn't sacrifice our entire race for his love. If he died, I'd follow soon after, and I would meet him in the Overworld."

Zylan had pushed the table toward Cael, stepping back and releasing a groan. "Please, don't do this, Cael. Not. Fucking. Her!"

"She will have a choice, but, Zy, we're losing. We need help, before there's no one left to help. You'll go check her out. That's an order," Cael had said, and he'd turned away from the table. Before leaving the room, he looked back to Zylan. "We would protect her as you protect my Fyrvor."

"Fuck your orders, Cael. If she dies, you will follow," Zylan had spat, backing away.

Zylan had watched the rest of the team scurry off. He hadn't been able to blame anyone for ducking out. The air had been too thick to breathe without leaving the sour taste of rage. Riam and Des had still stood at the table. Zylan had paused in the hall, secretly watching and listening to the only two people who'd have to pick up the pieces if this all went south. A long sigh had filled the meeting room.

"Well, that went better than I thought it would," Des had said, rolling her shoulders. "The tension in the room damn near stopped my heart."

Riam had taken a seat at the table, drinking down the rest of his beer. "It's not over yet, Des. You see how Cael is with you? Zylan doesn't have that control. Things are going to get bad. This was just the tip."

* * * *

After the events of the day, there had been only one thing to do. Zylan had hit the gym, as he had done each time his stress pushed him to the brink of homicide. He knew the Slayers had listened to him work out his anger in the gym many times. His screams tonight had echoed through the compound, bouncing into every room. His soon-to-be future had been chasing him since the day he'd left Sola-Nosfer. It'd scratched at his sanity, inch by inch. There had been no doubt in Zy's mind that everyone could feel his anger and, below that, his sadness and fear.

Now back in his bedroom, he collapsed. "My Fyrvor," Zylan whispered, holding on to a photo of his Neri, his Fyrvor.

Nerissa Sung was smiling in the photo, taken by Zylan, who had been pretending to take photos in the park where Nerissa had been having lunch in the sunshine. She was leaning forward. Her long, black, straight hair was draped over one shoulder. The sun kissed her hair as it kissed her skin. She was the most beautiful woman he had ever seen.

He and Neri had met several times at the Netherworld. She worked tirelessly on the dormant gene, trying to manipulate the active irregular gene. Her goal was to find a way to deactivate it. Her proposal carried a lot of weight with the Netherworld. Klers didn't waste their time on pointlessness. They always had a purpose. Her flavor of second sight was the future. Everyone listened to someone who could see the future. When a Kler was working toward something, the Netherworld gave them free rein.

If Neri could deactivate the gene, it would change the face of their war against the Rancor Order. The only irregulars left would be Vampyre. The Vampyre DNA wasn't part of the irregular gene. It was simply who they were destined to be. It was the same with a lot of the Therians. It wasn't an irregular gene that created all of them. They always had been and always would be.

Zylan curled up into a ball in his empty bedroom. He would tell Cael and the others about his fate later. For now, he would mourn. This was going to be what took his life. He would either carve out his own heart, leaving his love behind then become a husk of the man he wanted to be, or he'd keep his love and be hunted by his people. Either way, he would be dead. He wondered for a moment if Neri knew he was coming for her. Had she seen all of his wicked deeds? Would she hate him before he even knocked on her door?

Chapter Two

"Neri, are you coming?" a female's voice called out, pulling Neri's attention from her computer in the lab. "Doctor Sung? Neri?"

Neri sighed and tucked stray black strands of hair behind her ears. Her hair was poker straight, just like her mother's. Dr. Neri Sung was a first generation child in her family tree to be born off Korean soil, and she'd followed in her mother's footsteps. Both of her parents had been born and raised in Korea, but they had moved to Van City when her father was offered a job with the Netherworld Agency. Neri was a second generation molecular geneticist, like her mother, specializing in the irregular gene. And like her mother, she was usually engrossed in her work, to the point of neglecting her body's most basic needs. But tonight wasn't about work. Tonight was about survival.

"Not tonight, Beth. I'm running a few more tests. I'll see you tomorrow," Neri called back, not turning from her monitor. She knew she wouldn't see Beth tomorrow. She wouldn't see Beth ever again.

Neri rubbed her brow. It felt like dry sandpaper dragging across her sore eyes every time she blinked. On a good night, she was a workaholic, an addict. On a bad night, she was so captivated with finding a cure that she ignored her body's cries for sleep and food. She was the worst kind of addict. She loved her addiction. The only reason she slept was to store up more fuel to feed her work habit.

Neri waited for the office lights to click off. She was finally alone. Normally, she liked being alone here. She liked the silence. The offices of the Netherworld Laboratory were bustling during daylight hours. Her zone alone held over fifty personnel for the day shift and twenty during the night shift. Vampyres had this thing about working when the sun was beaming in on their labs. *Man, they're a demanding lot.*

Tonight was different. Tonight the uppity-ups were putting on a dinner for some random retiree, a Vampyre who she didn't know personally. Two hundred years bought dinner and a pat on the back. She thought it was odd, a Vampyre retiring. They had almost an endless supply of years. She couldn't see herself retiring willingly. She'd likely die at her monitor with a few test tubes in her hands.

Thankfully, all of the office blood drinkers were out in celebration, which left the office — and most of the building — empty. Any reason for the Vampyres to celebrate, and they were there. They were the life of the party, no pun intended. They regaled partygoers with stories from a time that could only be read about. The odd time she was forced to attend some Netherworld social, she enjoyed the stories most of all. It was the only thing she enjoyed about being away from her work.

Neri downloaded her work onto a thumb drive and packed her things into a small banker's box. Her files and life's work were reduced to one small white box. Being honest, her life in general was just tucked into that box. She *was* her work, and she never let anything else interfere with it. She lived alone, slept alone, ate alone and made her way through life alone. There wasn't room for more when her life consisted of living and breathing the cure for humanity. She had never planned to end up this way — alone — but there was little room for the hurt that would come from being left. She couldn't risk her mind focusing on something other than the cure. *Plus, how do I tell a lover that I'm running late and will be just another nineteen hours?*

She was ready to leave, and turned around, watching the clock. She did a mental check in her mind, remembering she'd forgotten to order flowers to be delivered to the workmate who was retiring. She knew she should have taken them herself or, at the very least, donated a bag of blood. But she wasn't a people person. She was a Petri dish person. And plus, giving flowers was lame, and giving blood was weird, even for her. Regardless, she had other plans tonight, plans she couldn't put off. Hell or high water, this was happening with or without her. She wished it wasn't, but fate didn't give a shit about her wishes. She'd read that in a fortune cookie somewhere. She was sure of it.

Nine on the nose, not as late as it usually was for her to be checking out for the night and leaving the office. She had a foldout bed in the corner and three changes of clothes, a toiletry bag and a stack of books for that very reason. She rarely got out of the office before midnight, if at all. She spent hours dissecting the irregular gene — researching the variations and trying to find ways to enhance or deactivate it, while factoring in the natural mutations that occur throughout generations. She had built off the foundation her mother had laid out years ago.

At the age of three, she had begun dreaming of the future. She had known this would be her life. She had known she would spend her days and nights working toward a cure. The only part she hadn't dreamed was if she would find the cure or die trying. From her dreams, she knew death would tap on her door a few times while she worked tirelessly to save mankind.

The pressure to show progress was overwhelming. The weight from above felt like a cockroach lodged in her ear, trying to burrow its way out through her brain. The Netherworld wanted a cure — and yesterday. She was close. She could feel it. She'd almost seemed to touch it with her fingertips a few times. But even if she'd found the cure, the natural mutations that occurred centuries ago had nothing to do with the irregular gene and would not be cured by any vaccine she'd create. Vampyres had been in existence prior to the irregular gene and gone unaffected by it. Therianthropy was a blood infection, not an irregular gene.

And when infected, the Therian virus killed the irregular genes within the body. There was room for only one beast.

Those with the ability to control with the mind, read the future, see the past, have superhuman strength and those who were classified by children as monsters... Almost all would be cured. No more claws and no more razor-sharp teeth. No more using abilities to dig around in the mind of someone else.

Part of Neri had mourned the outcome of a cure, as she was certain it would remove her own abilities. Maybe she was more hopeful than certain that being normal for once would be nice. Whatever the outcome, she was willing. For the good of mankind, she was willing to give up her own abilities. To keep people alive, to keep children safe, she would do a lot more than that. She'd end her own life for that cure.

She picked up her box and headed to the stairs at exactly four minutes past nine. She didn't take the elevator. It was too slow. Down six flights of stairs, she hit the lobby and pulled the silent fire alarm. It flashed on every floor, without the irritating scream that no one could think over the top of. The alarm would read on everyone's phones, computers and panic buttons that they were forced to wear while here. The highest level of the Netherworld made up each floor. All of their secrets had built this structure from the ground up.

After releasing the metal arm on the alarm, Neri walked out. Anyone left in the building had just over ten minutes to escape. That was double the time they'd need. She knew exactly how long it would take to leave. She had practiced the drills with them—countless drills over the years—and every new employee was trained accordingly. It took a maximum of five minutes to exit the building, even from the very top floor.

Loading her little red car with her white cardboard box, she pulled away to a safe distance. The building—which looked like every other building in the immediate area, minus any signage that gave the purpose of the place away—was leveled at exactly twenty-one minutes past nine. The explosion shook the block. Glass blew in all directions. Car alarms echoed down the street. Everyone for miles would be coming to see what happened.

It played out exactly as her dream had shown her. She had known this would happen, at this exact time, on this exact day, years ago.

As she pulled away, she remembered how her path had crossed with an undercover agent in a park. He'd taken pictures of the flowers and trees, but she knew he'd been taking pictures of her and that they'd met many times in various places. She had felt him watching her, but she wasn't afraid. Since meeting him, she had felt safer.

She knew he would come out of the shadows if she needed him. She could feel the affection he had for her. Somehow, he loved her. And in some odd way, she loved him back. He was her only friend—one she never spoke to or spent time with, shared stories or coffee with. But he was more of a friend than anyone else in her life. More than that, she knew he would be coming for her. The reasons were still unclear, but she knew she had to go with him.

She put her car in gear and headed to the safe house. It was a safe house for the Slayers. No one outside of the Genesys Project and their liaison with the Netherworld knew of its location except her. That was as far as her dream had taken her, to the front door of a broken-down cabin once used as a meth lab on the outskirts of the city, tucked behind Cypress Mountain. It was condemned, boarded up, and it had blood on the floor and walls from the last raid. The Slayers had taken it over, left it a shit-shack on the outside, but fortified it down below.

Driving with her radio on, she was calm. Her dreams always led her in the right direction. But in her calmness, she mourned the finale of those dreams. She would have no more visions in her dreams about this path. Her last dream of this night ended with her on the doorstep of the safe house. The rest was eaten up by darkness. It was never good when her dreams stopped cold. It usually meant the person in her dream was dead, and there was nothing left to tell. It was like closing a book. She hoped that in this case there would be a part two.

She could feel the darkness coming down to the very marrow in her bones. She had dreamed of this darkness. Always, in her dreams, she felt it behind her, like a shadow that she could never clearly see. A weight pressed over her body, something pushing down on her shoulders with nails that cut her skin. She breathed in a thick dread. She knew it was coming — the darkness — and it hungered for her pain. It didn't compromise. A ruling had been made.

Chapter Three

Zylan stepped into Cael's office, closing the doors behind him with sweaty palms. He had spent the last twenty-four hours holed up in his bedroom, curled up on the floor, staring into the darkness. He would have to bring his one true love back to the compound then leave her. He would abandon her in order to take on the duties of his birthright. It was that, or they all died. What was the point of any of this, if he was sentencing them all to death?

Cael glanced up from his desk, rubbing his fingers over his eyes. "Zy."

One word, clipped, tired, but ready for another round of *Too fucking bad, Zylan*.

Zylan pulled a metal folding chair from the back wall and plunked it down in front of Cael's desk. When he dropped onto the cold metal, the chair squealed in age. Zy's chest felt like someone had his heart and lungs in a death grip, allowing just enough blood and oxygen for him to survive, not tight enough for the sweet mercy of death. *Nope, I'm not that lucky*. It was just enough to be a constant reminder of the pressure cooker of a life he was born into.

"Cael, we need to talk," Zylan started, raising his hand to keep Cael from laying down the law again. "Don't worry. I'll bring Nerissa back to the compound as you ordered. This isn't about that."

Cael frowned, leaning back in his seat, arms across his chest. "Oh? What's this about then?"

Zylan took a few deep breaths, blinking his eyes to clear his unshed tears. "Where the fuck do I even start?" After a moment's thought and a deep breath, he said, "I'll start with my full name — Prince Zylan-Nefarious Bloodletting."

Cael's eyes widened. Clearly Cael had suspected ties, but not the kind that bound Zy by the throat. Little comments here and there throughout the years they'd spent together had told Zylan that Cael was close to the truth. "Heir to the throne of Sola-Nosfer?"

Zylan nodded, a small pathetic smile forming on his face. "In the flesh, for now."

"How old are you?" Cael asked, leaning forward. Cael knew. Being a lost boy without a society to call his own didn't mean he wasn't aware of the traditions. Everyone knew about the rituals and bullshit politics of the Vampyre society. "How much time do you have?"

"I have three months, give or take a few hours. In fewer than ninety days, I'm thirty." Zylan let out a deep sigh, his shoulders sagging forward. "When I was born, I was promised to a Vestal Virgyn. Amity-Rhuin Blooddawn, the daughter of a High Councilman."

"Fuck," Cael whispered, more to himself than Zylan.

Zylan's attitude lately probably made a lot more sense to Cael now, given that he was being auctioned off like a piece of meat, cattle for the slaughter. *At least the cow doesn't know the buyer has prime rib plans.*

"I left Sola-Nosfer when I was twenty. I was given ten years, less one day, and in three months, my time is up."

Cael shook his head. "We'll fight for you, Zy. If you don't want to go, we've got your back."

Sid, failed Watchyr, the master of perfect timing, stepped through the door. His face was as grim as theirs. "No can do, boss man. Anyone who attempts to keep royalty will be slaughtered." Sid clapped Zylan on the shoulder. "Sorry about your luck, mate."

Zylan gave a half smile. "Not as sorry as I am."

"Is there nothing we can do to help you?" Cael asked.

"My mother is sending Amity here for me to meet her. Y'know, before it all goes down. Are you cool with that?" Zylan asked, hoping Cael would say no but knowing he wouldn't.

"Anything you need, you've got it," Cael answered, in a voice that sounded like someone had kicked his dog. He looked to Sid. "What's up?"

"The Netherworld lab was leveled last night. The entire building came down." Sid turned to Zylan, as if he could read his mind. "Chill. Neri wasn't there. She was the one who pulled the alarm."

Zylan jumped up faster than his brain could process the information, grabbing onto Sid's shoulder until his balance returned. "Where is she? Is she hurt? We need..."

"Slow down, rock star. I tracked her into the back hills of Cypress Mountain. Our safe house was accessed at three this morning," Sid answered.

Zylan appreciated Sid having every stitch of information before stepping into Cael's office. Zylan stared at Cael, waiting for the go-ahead. He would have gone to Neri without it, sure, but he wanted someone to tell him it was okay. He wanted someone to give him the order to ignore the shit-storm of a birthright and the shitty future heading his way.

"What are you waiting for? Go get your Fyrvor," Cael said, standing up. "Take who you need, except Des."

Zylan smiled, nodding. Cael didn't let anyone take Des into harm's way unless he absolutely had to. It usually included an argument with Des, and she always won. She was a Slayer to the bone, and she was as fierce as any other member. There wasn't anyone who could keep that woman tied down. She was out in the field earning her feathers to pull her soul out of the chains in Hades. Cael had no backbone when it came to her. Zylan was the only one who didn't razz the guy about it, because he knew how it felt. His weakness was Neri, and he hadn't even spent one night with her.

Zylan had grabbed for the door when Sid stopped him. "Hold up, Zy. I'm not finished. Your little Virgyn is here."

"Already?" Zylan whispered, swallowing a rock-hard

lump in his throat.

"I can take care of the doll for ya, if you want?" Sid asked, grinning and giving him a wink.

Sid was a letch. He was one of the best Slayers they had. He had their backs no matter what, without fail. He could track like no one else — like a dog with a bone — and he didn't hesitate to take out a Proletaryan. But, to call a spade a spade, he'd sink his cock into just about anything and anyone. He wasn't picky. Hell, he was barely conscious when he was doing it. In Sid's case, the road to hell was paved in self-pity, self-hatred and self-harm. He loved only one — Des — and that was a stretch of the word.

Zylan froze at the door, staring Sid in the eyes. He may have hated the fact that he was being forced into wedlock with Amity, but he didn't hate her enough to make her endure a night with Sid. He didn't hate anyone that much. He wanted her gone but not like that.

"Zy, do you want me to take her off your hands, or are you going to deal with her? I can go to get Neri," Sid spoke again.

Zylan shoved his finger in Sid's chest. With a glaring look, he answered, "Do not fuckin' touch her. I may not like this shit, but if you lay your hands on her, she will be put to death. No piece of ass is worth that. Got it?"

Sid grinned, stepping back with his hands up in surrender. "Got it. Hands to myself. No sentencing the pretty little Virgyn to death."

Zylan pulled open the door, calling for Riam and a new recruit, Bane.

Zylan had worked undercover with Riam for what felt like years. Bane? He was new and had worked his ass off to get here. He was a Therian, a werewolf. He had perfect control of his animal, even while covered head to toe in blood and bits of people. With perfect marksman shooting, a steady hand, cool temper and whisper-quiet footing, Bane was the one Zylan wanted out in the trees keeping watch on his six. Bane had earned that respect, every step of the way.

Sid walked behind Zylan, looking back to Cael. "This is going to get ugly. You and I both know it. All of this… It's going to go south—and fast. You can't run from fate. Fate doesn't give room for personal choice. You can shape your destiny. Destiny gives you choice—left or right, forward or reverse, but fate is a one-way street. It's already mapped out. The choice is only an illusion. Fate doesn't give a flying fuck about your destiny, and destiny always leads you to the doorstep of fate. The fate that's coming is going to bend us over and fuck us hard."

Zylan ignored Sid then headed for his bedroom. He went through the motions, his mind a million miles away, thinking of his Neri. He put on his gear, piece by piece—robotic movements he'd performed night after night. His mind was filled with Neri, wondering if she was injured, safe or scared. He wondered if he could grab her and run. He knew it was wishful thinking, but the wish was nice to have, regardless.

"Ready to rock, Zy," Bane called to Zylan from the hall, metal on metal clashing as he jogged up.

Zylan snapped back from his foggy thoughts, grabbed his bag and pulled his door closed on his way out. Riam was following Bane.

"Sire," a small, fragile voice called out from the main hall ahead of him.

Zylan froze in his stride. Every muscle in his body seized, unmoving. He closed his eyes and growled. He went from being a man on a mission to a man with a problem—a really big fucking problem. Zylan's old world and new world had come to a face-to-face header. His body was torn between wanting to run and wanting to faint, vomit or scream. New was meeting old, and the feeling felt like a horse had kicked him in the balls.

Bane stepped out of the hall and into the meeting room then backed up, lifted his face and smelled the air. It didn't take any special abilities to smell the tension. "Zy, I think you have a guest."

Riam placed his hand on Zylan's shoulder, not needing to be told the story. Riam with no last name, always knew the story. "I'm sorry, my friend."

"I'm not following," Bane whispered from beside Riam.

"This is not my story to tell," Riam answered. "Zy, we'll meet you out front when you're ready."

Zylan stepped out of the hallway and into the almost-empty meeting room. Amity, a perfect specimen of a woman, filled the space as if she were completely suffocating darkness. She resembled a future he'd been running from. She was everything he didn't want. Being in the same room with her felt as if he were standing too close to a fire, and his body was starting to catch.

Zylan saw Amity drop to her knees, lower her face and wait. He understood that she waited for him to greet her or talk to her. She waited to be kicked, should he so choose to. She waited for a future that she was born to love and want and be proud of. She waited for something, anything. Whatever came her way, she was bred to endure and accept it without question. It angered Zylan that his people reared the consummate victims.

Her sheer white gown flowed around her, leaving nothing to the imagination. She might as well have been naked. Zylan knew that had he requested it, she'd have burned it while still wearing it. As delicate as she was, deep down she was trained to do some of the worst deeds known. She would kill for him at the drop of a dime. She'd do his bidding, whatever he wanted. If she was anything like his own mother, Amity was bred to be a tool, nothing more. His mother was relentless, cunning and more ruthless than even his father was. She'd had to be useful in order to survive.

My world is completely fucked up.

"Amity, there you are." Sid stepped into the room. Sid motioned to Zylan to speak, to do something other than stand five feet in front of her, staring at her like she had two heads.

Zylan cleared his throat. "Sid is going to keep you company, I have to go out. I'll be back later."

"Of course, Sire. Do you wish me to wait in your bedchamber?" Amity asked, keeping her eyes on the floor. Her voice was reserved, with a hint of fear that her training hadn't yet removed. That fear would stick around until her husband beat it out of her. Eventually, she would become used to the world and would welcome death. Death wasn't something a Vestal Virgyn feared, not when it was something that was prayed for. Eventually she would no longer fear him, as he would be the one to deliver the mercy of death.

"No. Sid will show you to your own room."

Amity nodded her head, eyes still on the floor. "I will wait for you there."

"No, I mean... Do what you want, Amity. This isn't a prison," Zylan said, finally giving up and walking away.

He gave Sid one last warning look then stepped out of the main hall. His steps turned into a jog then a full-out run. He had to get the hell away from her. His skin crawled. Being in the same room with her made him nauseated. The butterflies in his stomach were drunk on his nervousness and trying to crawl out of his belly button.

Zylan jumped into the 454 SS truck, Riam's baby. His body crawled and shook, making him fumble with the seatbelt. Riam didn't wait for Zylan to buckle up. He knew Zy would survive everything short of a head-on with a transport truck. Even then he'd come back as a full Vampyre. Riam punched the gas as soon as Zylan's ass touched leather. They were off to find Neri, towing behind them the one-ton load of regret stamped with Zylan's name.

Zylan knew he should have treated Amity better. His only wish for his mother had been that she'd been treated like a person and not an object to be used. But in that moment, he had done as his father had. He'd shit on her. His stomach rolled with each turn in the road. He was ashamed. For once, Zylan regretted how he'd treated a woman. Never once had he been that cruel to a female. Knowing how his mother had suffered had been the driving force behind his need to show even the smallest acts of kindness toward the opposite sex. But now he'd acted like the man he hated most, his father. He hung his head in shame.

Chapter Four

Strain took his usual back row seat at the Hemlock, tucked into the darkness. He was away from the prying eyes of the soon-to-be-dead irregulars who were dry humping to the shitty tunes blasting over the speakers. Gone were the days of good music. Now the speakers pumped with guitar music that sounded like a man having a seizure. But it was better than listening to the conversations that sounded even worse.

The brain dead had been debating world events, as if they'd had a fucking clue about any of it. He'd heard someone outside talking about feeding the homeless, as they'd stepped over a homeless man to buy some smack. Van City was hypocrisy at its finest. Those double standards were what kept him in business, so he didn't knock it that much. He did get a kick out of selling what amounted to an electric chair to them. With that, the circle of life would continue. The dead bodies of his last customers would be stepped over for the next asshole to buy.

He'd just finished up in the back VIP bathroom, pumping his own flavor of darkness into the hips of another fallen woman. Hookers... They were a dime a dozen around here. She'd given him little pleasure, most of which had only come at the end. He'd felt a small jolt of it when he pumped his load down her hungry throat. The dime bag whore had known what would come next—cash and H. This, like every other time, would have been the last time he had her. It had been the last time anyone would have her. After having tossed the H to the floor, he'd walked out, catching a glimpse of her scurrying around on the floor like a rat digging through the trash. As she'd thanked him, he'd shaken his head, like always. The last bit of humanity he still had left in him had always told the whore to leave the drugs and only take the cash.

"That shit will kill you," he would say, but they would never listen.

Soon he would own this shithole, and when he did, there would be changes. The music was on the top of his list. Décor would be number two. And as much as he loved watching his chemical in action, there would be no drugs being done on the premises. That was a heat score he didn't need. The continual flow of whores? Well, that would stay, only he'd make bank off their demise. There really was no better way to earn money. Like every other slimy bastard around, he'd make his cash off the suffering of others. Finishing his internal chuckle, he decided he'd keep a growing list of changes until he signed the papers and could start his teardowns.

With his rocks off and a drink in his hand, named after something toxic, he sat down. Every drink in this place was named after something tragic or poisonous. Sipping his drink of choice – a Narcissus – he got comfortable in his seat. Tonight he was celebrating the destruction of a Netherworld Agency lab. He'd carefully planned then personally set the charges that brought the lab to the ground. He didn't trust this job to just anyone. Scouting the building, plans and people for months, he'd brought the building to a crippling heap of rubble. He'd been disappointed that there weren't bodies littering the streets, but he'd take what he could get. Having a cure for the gene was the last thing the Rancor Order needed – well, at the moment.

His father's plans for an army hadn't panned out, but they still needed irregulars. His army was built up of irregulars. They weren't nearly as loyal as he'd wanted, but it was better than nothing. And until he no longer needed them, he'd slowly weed out the worst. He'd kill the rest when the job was done, not before. Without them, he'd be fucked.

Humans couldn't do the job. They weren't strong enough, physically or mentally, and loyalty was a word none had even heard of.

Each time he'd taken a human for questioning, he hadn't even had to touch them. They'd cracked on their way in, loyal until it no longer served them. They — like irregulars — needed to go. There was no room in this world for the weak, the traitors. They were the shit that stuck to the bottom of his shoes during his nightly street crawls.

He pulled out his cell phone and flicked back and forth. Each picture brought him back to the moment it had captured. He landed on a picture of Zoelle, best friend of Des. He had gotten off countless times to that picture. He would zoom in on the photo while he was balls deep in some streetwalking hustler. He remembered each scream. How sweet she'd been. Even if his father had almost lashed the flesh from his bones for it, he'd have done it again and again. He now wished he'd taken her and turned her, keeping her and pulling her out for his amusement.

He flicked his thumb to the side, landing on the photos of his new intended conquest. She was the only woman to make it out of the lab, with a white banker's box and a shuffle in her step. She had checked her watch several times between exiting the building and her car. She'd known it was coming down, and because of her, the death count was a glaring zero.

Nerissa Sung, molecular geneticist, had walked out of the building with minutes to spare. Strain had watched video surveillance of her survival. On her way out, she sounded the alarm system, warning the few stragglers in the building. Looking the last camera in the eye, she'd mouthed one word.

"Zylan," she'd whispered.

It would take Strain and his men a couple of days to sift through the footage. The Netherworld agents would be all over this — and her — within twenty-four hours. But Strain? He had plans for her. It would be one more jab from him at their new group. Oh, he had heard all about the Slayers. They could thank their own people and their weak mouths for that. It had taken but an hour, and Strain had what he'd needed from the last interrogation. Cael and his little band of flunkies had formed a group—the Genesys Project—to combat Strain and the Order. He had sent flowers and a card, congratulating them on their new promotions. His gift had been returned. *How rude.*

Strain looked up from his phone to see a man standing beside the table. "Garm, take a seat."

Garm, the new Calyph, replacing the traitorous Cael, took a seat in the club chair on the opposite side of the table from Strain. Garm, an irregular, was built like a brick shithouse. Standing six feet one, with shoulders that made Strain's look like toothpicks. Garm was perfect for the job. He was remorseless, slightly unbalanced in the head, didn't flinch and loyalty meant something to him. On several occasions, Strain had tested Garm's loyalty, and not once had he bent. He was willing to die for intel that didn't even matter. Garm was a keeper, for now.

"Hello, hun, what can I getcha?" The hostess with the mostest leaned into the table, looking at Garm, her bosom pushed up and flooding the top of her shirt, threatening to spill out.

"Nothing," Garm answered, not breaking eye contact with Strain.

Strain grinned. "He's good, but I'll have another."

She gave a nod and sauntered off. She, like ninety-nine percent of this club, was high as balls and barely touching the ground. Strain liked her, for some reason. She was quick on her feet, never asked questions and always cleaned up the back room when he was done. She wasn't left *special* tips—cash only. She could purchase her death somewhere else.

"Did you get my text?" Strain asked, knowing Garm had. He'd sent out a text demanding that Neri be found.

Garm gave a quick jerk of his head. "She's in some shack

on the backside of Cypress."

"I'd like her brought in tonight, unhurt."

"Already in process, sir. Dispatched seven of my best, under the explicit instruction that she is to remain unharmed," Garm answered.

That's what Strain liked most about him. Garm thought a few steps ahead, never overstepping but knowing exactly what was needed and when. Garm was a go-getter. Strain knew that eventually he'd have to kill him. Rising too far and too fast would be a problem when he'd come looking for another promotion. Strain would need to kill him or expand the operation. Strain was good with either decision.

"Well done." Strain smiled, lifting his glass and toasting the air.

With a nod, Garm stood and walked out. Small talk was not his forte. Strain appreciated that. Unless Strain was beating them to within an inch of their lives or fucking them to within an inch of their lives, he couldn't care for useless small talk.

With a new drink in his belly, Strain hit the streets. The desperation in the air prickled his skin. He stepped over the same homeless man he'd seen before and headed to his center. Newly purchased and soundproofed, with all the toys he needed to pry information from those who had the misfortune of meeting him.

Tonight he had another meeting. A little family get-together. And like most family meetings, it would be filled with wishing there was a way to kill them all and get away with it — or, at the very least, wanting to belong to a different family.

Meeting with his father, the Genesys, had reminded Strain of each time he'd walked into the middle of a gang turf war. It was a rush and was quickly accompanied with immediate dread, not knowing if he would walk away from it or die in a pool of his own innards. This would be much like the times he'd woken up next to a disgusting piece of ass. He'd known she was disgusting but had fucked her anyway. His regret and dread pushed his feet forward. Like that piece of ass, he couldn't ignore it or wish it away. Like the whore, he could only hope his father would leave quickly.

His father wanted to be kept apprised about the chemical, which was in mass production. He would also want to be updated on the release of the Proletaryans. Neither could exactly be flooded into the population. Inch by inch is what would win this war. Flooding the market with chemical would sound the alarms, and his little pet project would flop. He couldn't have the irregulars too scared to buy his product. Releasing all of his little creations would cause panic, and the streets would be littered with the po-po. His puppets weren't much help when there would be two cops to every one monster.

His father was impatient. He would feel that impatience on his hide. Hopefully he'd be able to walk after this meet and greet. He had shit to do, and healing wasn't on that list.

He couldn't fucking wait for his father to die. One day.

The inside of his new center looked like a sound studio. Little black egg cartons lined the walls, over layers of anti-vib padding — tried, tested and true. Someone could scream bloody murder and not a whisper could be heard on the outside.

Strain knelt in the back room — nude — and waited for his father. Each second ticked off, feeling like an hour dragging by. His father liked to build anticipation. He reveled in the fear Strain would be dripping in by the time he finally graced him with his presence. Strain couldn't blame him. He did the very same thing with those he took.

"My son," the Genesys finally spoke. His voice, as always, sounded like claws raking down the face of a chalkboard.

The room filled with the painful sound of his father's voice. Searing heat filled his eardrums, reminding Strain of the deep hate that was his father. Breathing in deeply and pushing his fists into the black mats under his knees, he waited. It took time for his body to acclimate to the insanity his father brought with him. His brain struggled between passing out and pushing forward. His father was an abomination, and sheer will alone was the only thing that kept Strain from bolting. He had to force his body to keep from entering survival mode, running from the impending danger.

The Genesys stood five feet in front of him, covered in the shadows of his own presence. Darkness surrounded him, forming the evil seed of a man that was the Genesys. Strain lifted his dizzy head, looking at his father with abhorrence and revulsion. He wanted to make his father proud, yet hated him for the limits his father placed upon him. His father, made of pure evil, was weak.

"Hello, Father," Strain spoke, unable to hold back the hate in his voice.

His father reached out of the dark fog, his boney white hand colliding with Strain's jawbone. The touch, never meant to be gentle, felt like an explosion behind his eyes. One touch was all it took for Strain to land on his side with the world ringing in his ears.

"You will learn your place or die, while you try to climb a ladder that isn't there," the Genesys whispered. The whisper filled Strain's head and pinged off his central nervous system. "You will do as you're asked. There is no alternative option."

Strain's stomach heaved. His father's anger touched every nerve and twisted around every organ. All he could do was nod as he tried not to vomit.

"Now tell me of your news, my good son."

Strain forced himself back into his kneeling position, his body feeling like melted jelly. His muscles threatened to give out, collapsing onto his shaking bones. Strain told his father of the Netherworld lab and of one escaped physician. He gave his usual update of the chemical and of his creatures.

"I have thought upon your suggestions regarding your puppets and the chemical. I will agree, for now. Planned attacks, as you put it, will do fine."

Strain nodded. He had implored his father to be

strategic—to think ahead—and he'd reminded him that times had changed. There were squads who worked tirelessly at keeping the irregulars above ground and out of body bags. Releasing all of the Proletaryans at once would end in serious bloodshed, but it would also end with the extermination of his puppets. They were easy enough to make, but it took too much time to rebuild an entire army. Cael and his band of misfits were taking them out too fast to launch a full attack. A flood of them would only cause a call in for more Slayers. More than that—being smart, crafty and ruthless was what would kick the Netherworld's feet out from under them. *Slow and steady wins the race.*

"Look further into these Slayers that I have heard much about, but be smart about it. Do not focus solely on them. To do so will be your ruin." These were his father's last words, which dragged across his brain like blistering daggers, before he fhaded from Strain's center.

The darkness that was the Genesys was gone. The fog filtered out of the little cracks and crevasses unseen to the naked eye. And with his father went the air, sucking away Strain's ability to breathe or blink. Falling to his side once again, he suffered, wrapped up in complete darkness.

One day, I'll kill my father and take his place.

Chapter Five

Cracking his knuckles, Zylan was jumping out of his skin, waiting for the truck to come to a stop. Hell, just to slow down a little, so he could jump. He was almost sure that Riam was taking corners on two wheels because he knew damn well Zylan would jump if he could. It took everything for him not to open his door and dive out anyway. He knew the truck would make it there faster, but at least he'd be doing something and not just sitting, twiddling his thumbs. It felt like he was letting her down in some way. Like if he wasn't running after her, it made him the reason for all of this. Love wasn't exactly logical.

His heart pounded in his chest. His thoughts were consumed with her. He swore an oath to her, silently, that if anything had happened to her, someone was going to die. At this point, he didn't care whose heart he ripped out — still beating — from their chest. As long as they slumped dead at his feet, he'd be satisfied. He honestly couldn't wait to get out of the truck. He needed the fight. He was in full combat mode and on the edge of insanity. Closing his eyes, he envisioned not just punching the SOB in the face, but punching through his face and brain. He clenched his fists at the thought. His knuckles throbbed to touch ground on a cerebral cortex or two.

Riam and Bane talked shop in the background, making a plan. For Zy, he didn't care what plan they had. He had one goal — Neri. He'd picked up bits and pieces of what they'd said, though. Bane would use his abilities to sniff out the area before they went in with guns blazing. Riam and Zylan would hold back a few feet, letting Bane scout. The idea of hanging back made him angry. He didn't want Neri to see Bane first. The thought blistered his ass. He should be the one to rescue her — only him. *She is mine.*

Zylan rubbed his sternum, trying to ease the tightness there. His world felt cramped, smaller than it had been when he'd thought his life couldn't get any worse. He'd sooner face his people and draw the Reaping blade across his own throat than have Neri in danger. Hell, he'd tap dance around the room and fill their celebratory glasses himself rather than this.

"Did you hear me, Zy?" Riam asked, nudging Zylan with his elbow.

Zylan blinked, staring at the clock. He knew they'd be pulling into the place in less than five minutes. He was thankful that Riam was behind the wheel. Riam knew the roads, inside and out. For once Zy had wished he had been full Vampyre, with the ability to fhade, dematerializing to any location he wanted. If the process didn't take so fucking long, he'd have cut his own throat back at the compound. But it went against everything his people had taught the younger Vampyres. No one fhaded into unknown locations, not unless they had a death wish.

Zylan rechecked his gear, double checking that he'd remembered extra clips, extra knives and a first aid pouch, just in case. It was all he could do to keep himself from imploding. He rotated his ankles, ensuring his boots were the right tightness for the full speed marathon run that was coming up in exactly four minutes. Rotating his head and shoulders, he was as ready as he was ever going to be.

"Zylan, you're a hair trigger away from losing your shit," Riam spoke up. "You need to ground yourself or you risk all of us. Try some deep breathing and…"

Zylan jerked his head to the side, meeting Riam's eyes, cutting him off. "Don't, not tonight, Riam. Not. Fucking. Tonight. Keep your therapy shit to yourself for once."

Riam's eyes grew darker, if one could possibly imagine a color darker than black. He slammed on the brakes, skidding on the loose gravel. He let go of the steering wheel and grabbed onto Zylan, pulling him by the shoulders to inches from his face.

"How the fuck are you going to save her if we're all dead? How the fuck does that help her? It won't. All it'll do is piss off whoever is chasing her. You'll be the death of her — of us all — and I'm not going to die for your bullshit. I won't die because you couldn't keep your shit tight."

Bane leaned back in his seat, taking a deep breath. "Usually I'm not one to chime in when you all throw down, but I suggest you kiss and make up. We're running out of time. I can smell it."

Riam pulled Zylan closer. "Tick-fucking-tock, Zy. I have all the time in the world, but she doesn't. What's it gonna be? Team up or team out, and you go it alone."

Zylan gave a few quick, jerking nods. "Team up."

Riam released Zylan and put the truck back on the road. Riam's shoulders relaxed, and his breathing returned to normal. Riam was the poster boy for meditation and tranquility. It was almost irritating. Zylan had never seen Riam lose his cool, not truly. Oh, he'd toss you the fuck on your ass and get in your face, but he'd never honestly lost his shit or his focus. Then again, to everyone's knowledge, Riam had never been in love. Love... Now that drug kicked him in the brain and stomped on his throat. It removed his higher reasoning and replaced it with sludge.

The truck went as far as it could go on the back roads. Zylan's heart skipped a beat. He was nervous. He feared she was dead. But he was also scared she was alive and that he would scare her even more than she already was.

Riam touched Zylan's arm. "We'll get her back, Zy, or we'll die trying."

Bane reached up from behind his seat. "Zy, you have my word. I will die before I give up on your Fyrvor, Slayer."

Zylan climbed out of the truck, his shaky legs surprisingly keeping him standing. They were restless, much like the rest of his body. The three men exchanged nods, then they were running, full speed. All three could book it like no one's business, but Bane was the fastest of them all. Bane would take the lead, clearing a path for Riam and Zylan. The location of the safe house was hidden from the world, tucked into the back of the mountain about two hundred yards off any beaten path. It would be a treacherous climb for Zylan and his two comrades, let alone the average Joe.

Following a climb that burned Zylan's legs, they were at their location. It was a single story cabin, a dilapidated eyesore that screamed a tetanus booster was needed. It had one window that was covered in plywood, a chimney that was falling apart and would lead to burning down the entire forest if someone tried to light it and a front door barely hanging on. But inside was a different story altogether.

Zylan had helped with the design—a small door in the back of the fireplace that led to a bunker. Below housed food and water, a two-way radio, first aid supplies, four bunk beds bolted to the ten-inch-thick steel walls and the odd book here and there. It could house half a dozen people for a week, more if you were in a crunch. Only a select group of people knew of this safe house, the Slayers, the Rector and Captain Salas Warner, who was their contact with the Netherworld Agency and the only one outside of the Slayers to know their intimate details. How Neri had found out about it was beyond Zylan. He'd never told her and knew no one else would have.

Coming to a halt twenty feet from the cabin, all three hunkered down in the brush and dirt. Each one of them had one task, and each would die carrying it out. Zylan watched Bane, eyes closed, breathing in the night's air. Zylan's skin prickled with goosebumps. The moon was high above them, not yet full. Zylan watched Bane shiver with each breath and new smell.

Zylan lifted his head to the tree canopies. Some of the oldest trees around stood above them, lending to their cover. Above the treetops, a crystal clear sky added just enough light for them to get their jobs done.

As Zylan stood, Bane grabbed Zylan's hand. "No!"

A beep-beep sounded, Zylan's ears twitched with the complete silence that followed. In less than a heartbeat, the forest exploded. The blast hit Zylan in the chest, blowing him back and into the trees that he'd just been admiring. On his back, his chest tight, he stared back up at the little diamonds in the sky. In that moment, it dawned on him how badly he'd wanted to do this with Neri—lie under the trees and watch the sky, for no other reason than to escape the world around them, to create a memory he could hold on to forever. It would be a memory that would carry him into his duty, a memory he could always turn back to, when the life he hated replaced the life he wanted.

Zylan could feel the darkness coming, seeping in and chewing away at his vision. He rolled his head to the side. The cabin was gone, leveled, erased from existence. His body felt cold, realizing the safe house was gone and with it, his Fyrvor—his reason to live, his reason to pick himself up off of the ground and keep moving. It took him a moment to realize his vision wasn't fading. It was blurred from tears. He felt them roll from the corners of his eyes.

"Zy!"

He rolled his head again, looking into the darkness of the forest. He saw Des, running full throttle, dressed in head-to-toe gear. Behind her, the Slayers followed, all of them suited up and ready to rock. Goosebumps covered his skin. They were here. They were here to help him rescue his Fyrvor.

Des skidded on the ground, grabbing Zylan's head, leaning over his face. Des was a thing of beauty, the kind of beauty you find in a raging inferno or in a wave that takes out everything in its path. There's always beauty in destruction and horror. You just had to look for it—like how a fire destroys but creates new life.

"Neri," Zylan finally spoke, his throat feeling like someone was standing on it.

Bane crawled over to Zylan, fresh wounds bleeding down

the side of Bane's face. "She wasn't in there, Zy. I swear to you. She's not here."

Riam, who was clean of wounds and debris, held his hand out to Zylan. Riam knew it was coming, and in true Riam fashion, he never disrupted the predestined path. There was no point in arguing with him about warning them. Riam didn't budge. He and Sid understood each other like no other could. Neither of them spoke of the future or gave warnings. They did what they could, in the only ways they could.

Zylan knew that Riam stopped the truck for only one reason. It wasn't to calm him down. It was to buy enough time to save the three of them. Riam did what he could.

Zylan took Riam's hand and stood, his knees needing a few chances to lock and keep him standing. He clapped Riam on the shoulder and gave him a nod, an unspoken thank you. The others bled out of the trees, having inspected the grounds around them.

Bane smelled the air. "You good to go, Zy?"

Zylan nodded and cleared his throat. "Can you smell her?"

"Them... I can smell them. The Order has been here," Bane answered and pointed toward the left, behind what was once the safe house.

"How did they know about this place?" Zylan asked, wondering the same thing they had all been whispering about.

"Neri's car that we found a few miles back... She took the side route. Her GPS was still active," Sid answered, pointing off into the trees and the direction of Neri's car. "Once they found her GPS signal, the rest would have been fairly easy."

Cael stepped forward and divided them into teams. They would stick together as they climbed off the mountain. Once Bane had a direction, they'd rip the city apart trying to find her. They would each take a district and work from there. It was all they could do for now.

Zylan was off and into the trees. He didn't wait for anyone. As much as he appreciated the Slayers all showing up in an effort to find his one true love, he couldn't hang back. He couldn't do anything but run. He couldn't have stopped his feet, even if he'd wanted to. Neri was with the Order. He didn't even want to think of what they were doing to her. He was a man on a mission, and he would take out anyone who stood in his way.

Bane ran at his side. He didn't ask questions or offer any warnings. He ran with his fellow Slayer, guiding their direction. Bane was good for that, falling in line and keeping his eyes forward. He would ignore the smell of fear pulsating off Zylan. He would ignore the salt taste of tears in the air. It was guy code. Tears and fear always went unnoticed. Push on, no matter who was crying or shaking like a leaf.

Zylan and Bane were lost to the wind, full speed ahead. Zylan would get his Fyrvor back. He had to. Anything less would end him completely. *How can I live in a world that doesn't have her? How can I protect a world that doesn't include her?* He couldn't. He wouldn't. Her death would be his true death.

Chapter Six

Still weak from his meeting with Father Dearest, Strain sat in a plush, black leather wingback chair with a glass of bourbon in his hand. The ice jingled against the crystal highball glass as he swirled the booze around the cubes. Now that he'd relieved his anger from meeting with his father on some poor soul, he sipped his well-earned drink.

The compound was silent and not just because of the soundproofing he'd had installed here to match his center, but because he had sent everyone away. The soundproofing wasn't as big a deal around these parts. The compound was located at the end of Blood Alley, where no one dared venture. Those who did come around these parts wouldn't have given a rat's ass about noise of torture or screams. No one came down here unless it was for nefarious acts, to be played out by those who didn't need the heat. It was the perfect site. Hope and righteousness didn't live around here.

He was pleased, as usual, with Garm and his game hunt. Garm, as he'd promised, had dropped Nerissa at Strain's feet. Neri was a little banged up—her doing. She'd run. Then when she couldn't run fast enough, she'd fought. But for the most part, she'd been delivered unharmed. He was delighted. Pleasing Strain was a difficult task on a good day, let alone after a run-in with the Genesys.

Strain was a perfectionist like his father. He liked everything to be a certain way and executed in a particular manner. Garm toed the line, performing tasks exactly how Strain would have wanted. Garm was a step ahead, predicting exactly what was to be done and how.

In a chair—the same as Strain's—Nerissa slumped, unconscious. Her head lolled to the side. He didn't bother with restraints. There was no way out. If by some miracle she did get out she wouldn't make it very far. She'd be dragged down some side alley and killed before finding a soul, literally. Souls came here to die, not to be saved. As disgusting as this neighborhood was, it had its perks.

The room smelled of previous visits. The walls were stained with fear and blood. No amount of bleach would get that kind of vomit and death out of the air. He didn't mind the smells, though. He enjoyed the aroma just before someone died. It was delicious. It added to the thrill of the next, hinted at what was coming. The smell of new and old was exhilarating. He could spend hours in here, eyes closed, savoring every memory.

Strain shivered, breathing in deeply. His cock reared to attention. He stood, moving closer to Nerissa Sung. Her bone structure was like a delicate porcelain doll's. Her Korean features reminded him of movies he'd watched as a child. She looked like someone who should be on billboards and not behind a microscope. Her jet-black hair, twisted into knots, hung over her shoulder. He smoothed out the little hairs around her bruised cheeks. Tiny lines under her eyes said this was probably the deepest sleep she'd had in weeks.

This tiny package held so much promise. It was his experience that the smaller ones gave the biggest fight. Perhaps being the smallest throughout life had forced them to fight for every inch they'd gained, or maybe it was that they were harder to hold onto. They wormed free easier than the fat and plump ones could. The fat ones tired so easily. They were no fun.

He was looking forward to Nerissa waking up. For now, he'd let her sleep. He wanted her in tip-top shape, rested and ready for round one. He liked them feisty.

Taking his seat again, he grinned. He was hopeful the blast that had taken out the safe house had taken out a few Slayers, but he wasn't about to bet the farm on it. The Slayers had horseshoes stuffed up their asses. They always managed to make it out alive.

Giving credit where credit was due, they owed it all to Cael. He didn't train bitches. Cael trained warriors. He trained the best of the best. They all gave Strain a run for his money, and he'd have it no other way. This conquest wouldn't be worth it unless he had to work for it. Victory was much sweeter when one had to claw your way to the top on the backs of those one had been better than, stronger than, quicker than.

The Slayers were like sewer rats. The only thing to do was set traps and hope they were stupid enough to step into them. It only took once. Just one wrong step, one wrong turn, and snap, the trap would come down on their necks. One by one, he'd take them out.

Zylan... Strain knew of him and his family. The little Prince, Zylan-Nefarious Bloodletting, was born as cursed as Strain. Both of them were born heirs to a throne. The only difference? Zylan didn't want his throne, and Strain did. Taking out Zylan would be a blow to the Vampyre society. Taking Nerissa was a two-for-one deal. The intel he could gain from Nerissa would give the Order the leg up they needed, and, in turn, killing her would end the little Prince. Zylan was one of Cael's closest. Ending him would kick Cael in the nuts.

Love breeds stupidity, among other brain ailments. Zylan would come looking for Strain, love-drunk and making enough mistakes for the rat trap to snap across his throat, ending his life. Strain's father would be proud. He knew it.

Nerissa moaned, groggy, sending a scorching pulse down the shaft of Strain's cock. He breathed in deeply, exhaling with a shuttering moan. He pulled open the zipper of his pants, releasing his throbbing dick, palming himself at the thought of triumph—one more stab at the Slayers, one more shot at his traitorous brother.

Holding his hardness, he wouldn't allow himself release—

not yet. He would draw out his own suffering as he drew out hers. It would make his release so much greater. He would force himself to earn his pleasure. Later — much later — he would pump his hateful hips into her insufferable body after turning her into another puppet at his command.

Strain laughed, the sound bouncing off the walls, filling the room with a dark hate. He had special plans for Neri. Each one of those plans would make her wish she'd have remained in that building as it had come down.

The darkness was arriving. All he had to do was open up and let it out.

Chapter Seven

Neri sagged in the corner, pressing her bruised back into the black Styrofoam egg carton wall that kept her screams and the stench of death locked inside this room with her. Each scream would end with her gagging over the smell of those who'd never left the room on their own two life-filled feet.

Her attacker, known to her and the agency as Strain, would come and go, kicking her like a dog, as he pleased. He was easily amused and just as easily angered. He waffled between sanity and absurdity, completely losing touch with reality. At first, she'd prayed he'd slip completely into deranged and would begin to make mistakes, but each time he licked that fine line, he'd come back swinging.

She'd hung for the last hour, tied to the wall with her blood slowly draining out of the small wounds on the backs of her knees. They'd nicked the popliteal artery that branched off from the femoral artery. She'd thought she would have bled out sooner, but, to her surprise, it wasn't working out as she'd begun to pray it would. Dangling by the wrists, she wondered how long it would be until she would finally just die.

Not soon enough…

That surprised her more than anything else, how resilient her mind and body could be when pushed to the brink. She'd thought to herself how great a paper this experience would make. Passing time, she'd thought of a solid argument for psychological warfare and what would and would not work to break a human being, along with the length of time it would take. Being an irregular, she wondered if that played a factor in the length of time it took for her to die.

Days of interrogation and torture had passed, him asking the same questions over and over, and each time she wouldn't answer. She had the answers, through dreams and second-hand knowledge, gossip and the very little information she'd been given on a need-to-know basis. He'd asked about the banker's box he'd seen her leaving with. She wouldn't tell him. She wouldn't tell him anything, including her name. He already knew too much. She'd known that he'd been watching her. But his own knowledge was limited to what any hacker could find out. He—like many others—could have hijacked the camera feed and watched her walk out of the building.

Her mind was a steel trap. Nothing was going to open that door, not even the death she was hanging from the wall waiting for—the death she prayed was coming. Eventually, it would. She was getting weaker with each drip of blood. There would be freedom and peace in her death, and she welcomed it with open arms.

Something about his frustration with her had pleased her. He'd tried everything, next to finally killing her, but she wouldn't break. He couldn't make her talk, and it pissed him off. It wasn't out of strength that she didn't break. It was fear. Fear was a strong motivator—stronger than any ounce of strength her mind could muster. Fear was her power, and nothing he could do would remove that power.

Strain's frustration was marked on every inch of her flesh, layer over layer. The bruising blackened her alabaster skin. She was usually pale, but lately, due to starvation, sleep deprivation and torture, she was pastier than normal. Staring down at her nude body, she giggled. At first she laughed to herself, the hysteria finally breaking over and flooding the room.

"I look like a Dalmatian," she giggled to herself, looking down at her spots.

She shook her head. She was finally certifiable. She'd hit complete madness. She knew she wouldn't find peace in death any time soon, but she'd find peace in lunacy. Complete psychosis was just around the bend, and she couldn't wait. At least she wouldn't be aware of what he was doing to her body. Perhaps it was blood loss, or perhaps this is just what happened to people held captive and tortured.

She'd read stories of people who had gone mad in war camps, their minds no longer able to tolerate the assault. Once wondering how it took hold of the mind, she now knew. For her, it wasn't a quick happening. She hadn't opened her eyes to a complete destruction of her mind. She'd felt it slowly creeping in. Unhurried, the madness came to her, and she welcomed it. She didn't fight to remain aware and sane.

Her internal insanity had taken time to set in. The first day had been painful, but after he'd leave, she would recite the genetic sequence of every species she knew. She'd moved onto things as trivial as the periodic table or listing the ingredients of her favorite dishes her mother had made her. She missed her mother, who'd died of a lonely heart. After her father, an agent for the Netherworld, had passed, her mother had raised her into adulthood. Once she'd known Neri would make it, she let herself go home, to her mate.

She'd pulled her mind from her mother, never remaining there for too long. Too long made her sad. Instead, she'd recite the Hippocratic Oath or list every instrument she would need to perform a specific task in her lab.

Neri's body didn't seem to want to give up, as much as she pleaded with it to abandon life. *Who the hell can take this kind of treatment and still wake up?* Since her body was alive and thriving in this condition, she could only hope her mind would go quickly. But it hadn't come quickly. To her dismay, it had taken a lot to snap her reality.

On day three, she'd known no one was coming for her. There would be no rescue. Thinking back to packing her banker's box, she'd thought about getting a message to Zylan, but she didn't know how. On her way to her car, she'd looked directly into the security camera and mouthed his name. She knew someone would see it. She'd left the GPS on in her car, so someone would know where she was heading. Downside was that's exactly how Strain and his maggots had found her. And now, after almost a week, the thought of a rescue was as ludicrous as him opening the door and letting her go.

The days bled into each other and no one came, besides the monster who abused her for information they both knew she'd never give. What made things worse? She knew he was hoping she wouldn't spill. He'd begun to look forward to each and every time he came to visit her. This wasn't about intel. This was about some sick fuck getting off on each bone that snapped and echoed in this room of disgust.

Knowing she was on her own didn't make her slide deeper into a pool of self-pity, though. It gave her power, a sickening power. Strain's frustration with her unbending will gave her satisfaction unlike anything she'd ever felt. To be fair to herself, she'd never been in this kind of situation before, where she took joy where she could.

Her life had been sheltered. Her mother had worked every day of her life, yet had always found time to be a parent. She had been private schooled, had had friends and a modest home that had been filled with love. There had never been a day where she'd felt neglected or unloved. Her mother had been busy, but she'd made a point of teaching Neri how to make it in a world that didn't care if she was dead or alive. That was the blunt truth of the world — a truth she learned early, before both parents were gone.

That truth had been what pushed her to endure. The world didn't care about her wounds or her cries of pain. The world was going by, with or without her. She would make sure her mark in this little hellhole of a world, would forever be stained on the walls and on the half-eaten soul of Strain. He would remember her for all time. He would remember her mocking smile and hear her laughter when he stripped down to a hard-on. She would bruise him in any way she could, because the world didn't give a shit about him either.

The cruelty she showed him was minor compared to what he could dish out. Once, she was a doctor, a daughter, a friend, a person, and now, she was thriving on the cruelty she managed to serve up. She was losing who she was, bit by bit. Neri said goodbye to who she was and welcomed the woman she'd have to become. Once the type to step over a spider and nurse a bird, now she'd become the type to shove that bird down his throat. As long as Strain was suffocating on it, she wouldn't flinch as the bird died.

Lifting her head up, she whispered, "Orygin, I pray to you. Please allow me the release of death. Welcome me home. Let me leave my broken body behind, nurse my mind and soul in your arms, soak my brokenness in the pools of Elysium. Strain is never going to let me go. I fear the pain will be so great that I will bring shame to my family. The deeds of this prison have brought shame to my father's name. Please, allow me to leave this place. Allow me to restore the dignity of my family."

It had been many days since she'd felt anything besides paralyzed emotions. Letting go of the initial panic had been easy. Feeling it creep back in felt like another crushing blow.

"Please, let me come home. Welcome me into Elysium," Neri whispered. Then she pushed her face into her arms as she cried. "Tell Zylan I know that he looked for me. Tell him he did his best. Watch over him. He'll need you."

"You bring no shame to your family. You bring honor and respect," a man's voice spoke to her. *"It'll be over soon."*

She jerked her head, looking around the black Styrofoam-walled room. No one was there. For days, this voice had spoken to her. He hadn't said anything of great importance. Sometimes she could feel him holding her hand, and sometimes he told her stories of a place stuck between sunrise and sunset. She told him stories of her childhood, and he told her stories of a woman named Desdemona. He'd told her that he didn't have a childhood. He was born and matured, then planted beside Desdemona to keep her on a righteous path. He would never answer her questions about her fate, only tell her that the torture would end soon.

"Close your eyes now, Nerissa," he said. *"I'm here. You're not alone. This is almost over."*

Neri nodded, scalding tears rolled from her eyes, leaving blistered trails on her puffy cheeks. *Are my prayers finally being answered? Is this it?* The tears rolled faster. She would never finish her life's work. She would let her people down. She wouldn't save them. She prayed that her banker's box, tucked behind boxes in the safe house, would be found. Someone could continue her work. Someone could save them all.

The creak from the door made her stomach pitch and try to jump out of her throat. She would have vomited had there been anything in her stomach. They'd tried to feed her, but she wouldn't eat. She'd hoped she'd starve to death. At the time, that thought made her grin. All of this work, just for her to starve, and Strain would lose his little lost puppy to kick.

With panic just under her skin, she steeled her emotions. She told herself that Zylan could still be searching for her. She knew he loved her. She knew only death would keep him away from her. She thought of each time he tried to be casual and cross paths with her, how nervous he looked when he'd give her a nod.

She could see him, the memory of him in her mind's eye, standing six feet tall, buzzed hair, covered in tattoos and piercings. He looked like a bad guy until he spoke. His voice was calmness, safety and with a firm promise of duty. His eyes were hard at first, until he focused on her. Tuning out the world, his eyes bled into something closer to a pool of compassion and trust.

"Neri!" Zylan's voice echoed through the room, the force sending her into brief panic. Was she imagining this? Had she finally gone completely bonkers? Or was she finally dead, and this was her Elysium?

Neri risked opening her eyes, thinking she was hearing things. Zylan was coming toward her like a freight train. He was covered in blood, his men at his back. Neri broke. Her body vibrating, her cries became louder at the complete relief she felt the moment she saw him.

Zylan cut her down and fell to his knees, pulling the shirt from his back and covering her naked and battered body.

"I knew you'd come," she whispered, reaching up and touching his check. "I knew it."

Zylan picked her up then pulled her into his chest, standing with her frail body in his arms. Neri winced in pain, but she clung to him. Stepping out into a hallway, Neri grabbed the door frame.

"There's another woman. She's in here. They have another woman," Neri said, trying to keep him from taking her farther out of this dungeon.

"Riam!" Zylan called out. "She says there's another woman being held here."

A man who looked too pretty to be a warrior stepped forward. That wore off the moment you looked into his eyes. Neri tried not to flinch when her eyes met the handsome Slayer, Riam.

"I'll take another look, but we have to go — now. Backup is coming. We can't fight them all, Zy," Riam spoke. Neri and Riam made eye contact again. This time Neri didn't recoil. He gave her a nod and left their side.

Neri tucked her head into Zylan's chest as he ran down the hall. She could hear screaming and guns sounding off with the arrival of backup. She prayed they all got out alive. To die now would be too great an insult.

Behind them, she could hear Riam. "I'll come back for you. I swear. I'll come back for you."

"Run!" the woman screamed from the back. "Get her out of here!"

Out of the side door, Neri and Zylan went down in the dirt, bullets flying over their heads.

"Give me a gun!" Neri screamed to Zylan.

"Can you use one?"

"Give me a fucking gun," she barked. "I was just rescued. I'm not going to fuckin' die out here now."

Zylan passed her a nine-millimeter—not her personal choice, but it would do. It was one of Des' spares, he'd said as he'd passed it to her

"Des is my field partner," Zylan said. "I always carried a spare for her."

Pulling the shirt over her body, it falling to her knees, Neri belly-crawled behind a dumpster. Taking a deep breath as her father had taught her, she aimed and eased on the trigger. Her father had taken her to the range every weekend until his death. With every bullet she fired, she thanked her father for teaching her skills she had never thought she'd need.

Three clips later, Zylan and Neri had cleared a path for the other Slayers. As Zylan's people flooded out of the back door, Neri's legs wobbled. She'd lost too much blood. She grabbed onto Zylan, the world spun and she was done.

Chapter Eight

"I don't understand the concept of this game," Amity said, staring at the pool table. "We hit the hard balls with a stick, sending them into little bags, but why? I do not understand the point. They all go into the little bags then we take them all back out and start over. That's the very definition of insanity. Doing the same thing over and over, expecting different results."

Sid laughed, explaining the game of pool to her again. He'd spent the past week entertaining Amity for Zylan, who was out day and night in search of Neri. Zylan would return only to eat, stock up his gear, doze for an hour or two then head back out. Amity didn't ask questions about his comings and goings. She stayed behind, as she was directed, and she waited.

"So, we do not expect a different result? Why ever would we continually remove the balls from the bags if that is where they are to be?" she asked, frowning. "I'm still confused about this game."

"Don't they have games back where you're from?" Sid asked her, taking a shot and missing. He was a pool shark, but he was giving her a chance. He liked to draw out the game. He enjoyed spending time with her. Amity wasn't like the others. She hadn't grown to hate him or begrudge him for his abilities and lack of reactions. He was Sidriel — nothing more and nothing less. She didn't question why he wasn't out there, pointing to Neri's location. The others had. Riam was the only one'd who kept Zylan from skinning Sid alive.

Amity shrugged. "Games? Of that, I'm sure. Alas, Vestal

Virgyns do not engage in such things. We are not permitted to play games. We were not made for that reason. Of course, we would be trained in any sport of our mates, in case they wished to play."

"You were not made. You were born. You're not a thing, Amity. You're a being," Sid corrected her. He hated that she referred to herself as an object.

Amity blushed, as she usually did when he made her a person and not a thing to be taken out and used, as you would a pencil or a hunting dog. Even then, a hunting dog was respected, treated kindly, and not used like an object. Her pink cheeks made her a little more beautiful to Sid.

Over the days, Sid had finally convinced her to change out of her gauze gowns into leggings and a shirt. Her long white-blonde hair was pulled into a tight braid and exposed her face. When no one was looking, he caught her staring at herself in a mirror, as though she had never seen her reflection before. This world was obviously brand new, and although it had scared the hell out of her, it had also intrigued her. Sid had been with her almost every step of the way. At first he saw it as a hassle. Now he looked forward to it.

Amity tilted her head and frowned, turning her head toward the front room. Sid had felt the same rush of energy coming this way.

"Something is wrong with Zylan," Amity whispered, rubbing her chest. She placed her hand on the pool table, dropping her cue with a clatter. She tried to take a deep breath and struggled. "Sidriel, something is wrong. Can you feel it?"

Sid moved to her side. "Zylan has found Neri."

Amity nodded. "Zylan loves her very much, yes?"

Sid nodded. He didn't want to answer out loud. He felt bad for Amity and didn't want to tell her that she was not the object of Zy's affection.

"Do me the honor of truth, Sidriel. He doesn't want this arrangement with me, does he?"

"No, he doesn't. But he will honor it. Out of duty and respect for you, he will," Sid answered, trying not to feel sorry for her.

"I have been prepared for a marriage that is unwilling. I was taught, but I did not know I would feel this way about it," Amity whispered, her face falling. She looked disappointed.

"Feel what way?" Sid asked. She schooled her emotions so strongly that Sid had difficulties reading her.

"Badly, as though I am doing something wrong. I was taught about force and acceptance of it onto me, but never onto my mate."

"Force, either way, is wrong. I don't care what your books told you." Sid could feel anger building in his gut. *Backwood hicks, the lot of them.* They still believed in marrying into the same family, to keep their bloodlines as pure as possible. Purity didn't breed strength. It bred an extra arm, eighteen toes and gills.

"I can feel something else," Amity said, twirling her fingers in the air. "Darkness... I can feel darkness coming."

Sid let his anger go, opening himself up to what Amity was feeling. "Neri... She is close to death."

Amity went to lift a gown she wasn't wearing. Blushing, she stepped forward. "We must go to them at once. Together we can help them."

Sid stepped back, lifting his hands. "I can't. I can't help."

Amity stopped dead in her tracks and turned. "Sidriel, you and I had an agreement. There would always be truth between us. Do not tell me you cannot stand beside me. Do not tell me you cannot be there for your fellow Slayers. You may not be able to save her, but you can be there for Zylan, as he will not want me to comfort him. You will help, in whatever way you are allowed. Do not be a... How did you say it? Yes, a yellow belly."

Sid grinned. He'd called her a yellow belly when she'd been too scared to step out of her room in pants. But he had to admit that this time she was right. With a nod, he followed Amity at a dead run into the back infirmary.

The room, set up as a miniature operating room, was filled to the rafters with Slayers. In the middle, Zylan had Neri on the table. Riam and Cael worked to keep her alive.

Zylan turned to the door as Amity and Sid burst in and pushed their way to the middle. He pointed from Sid to Amity, "You, get her out of here. *Now*."

Sid touched Amity on the shoulder, trying to stop her from moving forward. "You heard the man."

Amity pulled her shoulder from him and looked Zylan directly in the eyes. Something she never would have done—or should have done. She was to follow his rule at all times or suffer. Looking as if she'd instantly grown a backbone, she straightened her shoulders and pressed on.

"You may beat me to death later for this. I will bind myself to a bench after oiling a belt, for your arm to swing down upon my nude and waiting body. I will even thank you for each lash and nurse you should you need a rest from splitting my skin wide open to the world, my sire. But in this moment"—Amity moved closer toward Sid—"you need me to save your Fyrvor. Without me, she will die and return as a darkness you will need to destroy. If this is what you truly wish, I will take my leave, but I will not suffer your wrath upon my body later when you must burn her and her darkness."

Sid was right beside Amity and touched her on the shoulder. "Zylan, she is offering what we cannot do. She is offering what I'm not permitted to do. Give her the chance."

"We must hurry. Each moment we wait is a moment that brings her closer to darkness," Amity spoke boldly.

Zylan glared at Amity. "If you hurt her…"

"I know. You will kill me," Amity finished his sentence and turned her back to him. She moved to the table, looking to Cael. "I have read texts of this darkness. A force called the Order is creating an army of darkness. We have but one chance. Stitch her up. The rest of you come closer. I will need your energy."

Sid watched everyone carefully for a response, but no one asked questions. Cael kept stitching the wounds on her wrists and backsides of her knees. He stitched quickly, as everyone else moved forward.

Amity didn't bother looking to Zylan. "Sire, please come touch my shoulder. Everyone must touch. We will use your love for her to bring her back to us."

Zylan looked like he didn't want to touch her. Sid could sense his reluctance.

"Touch your Fyrvor. If you cannot bear to touch me, touch her. There can be no ill feelings involved," she said then looked to Sid. "Catch me when I fall."

Sid gave her a wink. "Eight ball, corner pocket... You've got this one."

Amity smiled, her eyes glittering with tears. She looked toward Zylan. "I am truly sorry for this, sire. I did not know you already had a love. I'm sorry for coming."

Sid stepped up behind Amity, touching her hips to steady her. He knew this could kill her. She was willing to die to save the woman her promised mate loved. "If you do not make it, it has been a true honor to have met you, Amity."

"Wait! What do you mean, if she doesn't make it?" Zylan spoke, but it was too late.

The room burst with the heat pouring from Amity. Tilting her head to the ceiling, she screamed as the blistering wave left her body and wormed its way into Neri, searching. Watching her with her eyes squeezed shut, Sid could feel her jerking in pain. He knew Amity had sent her mind into Neri to search for the invading darkness. It was something Sid was strictly forbidden to do, for any reason. A path could never be interrupted by a Watchyr. But no one said anything about a Virgyn.

Sid closed his eyes and followed Amity's soul as it traveled into Neri. At the core of Neri—a place deep inside and safe from the world—her soul was cornered, fighting for life. Amity pushed her heat into the darkness, pulling Zylan's love with her. The love, in turn, lit the way, forcing the darkness to retreat, forcing it from its painful grab onto Neri's soul.

Sid continued to watch, enthralled, as with one last push — with everything Amity had — she shoved it all into Neri's heart. One final push and Neri's heart fluttered like a caged bird. The deep corner inside Neri lit up like the fourth of July. Amity sliced off a piece of her own soul and gently set it inside Neri, giving her enough to hold on to. With a spark of life, Neri's soul shoved Amity from deep inside. Sid was tossed out with her. Neri's soul was now strong enough to fight off invaders.

Sid admired Amity and how she hadn't paused to think about herself — or that she'd be giving Neri a piece of her own soul. She hadn't stopped to think about her death or that she was saving the one person who stood between her and Zylan.

Once Neri's soul had felt Amity's invasion and they'd both been ejected from within her, the force threw Amity back from the table. She lifted off the ground with Sid holding on behind her. Zylan came running as she landed on top of Sid, reaching out to her.

"You did good," Sid whispered, holding onto her.

Amity smiled and turned her face to Zylan. "I did what a Vestal Virgyn could only hope and pray for. I've pleased my sire. It is a good first death, my sire."

Sid pushed Zylan's hands away from Amity. "You don't deserve to hold her in her last moments."

Sid felt the weight of Amity's decisions pushing down on her failing heart. She did as any Vestal Virgyn had dreamed about. It was the highest honor she could ever have. She had done an unasked task that had given her sire honest happiness. At least this knowledge would make her walk into her next life. A journey free of burden and curse. Sid knew Amity would die her first death willingly, knowing her sire would be happy. It was the Vestal Virgyn way, always on the edge of the blade, ready to plunge it into their hearts if it made their mates happy.

Sid moved into her vision. "Corner pocket... You got it."

A small laugh escaped her lips. "In your face, yellow belly. Game over."

Sid placed a small kiss on her forehead, a lump forming in the back of his throat. "No cheating. Game isn't over until the fat lady sings — two lives, no cheating."

Amity nodded. Sid watched as her first death crawled into her body to take up residence. There would be no pain, even though many thought there was. This being a death she'd chosen, it would give her the peace she needed not to fight it and just let go. If she hadn't damaged her heart beyond repair, she'd return as full Vampyre. If she'd given too much, there would be no return for her. In a way, Sid selfishly hoped there would be no return for her. He didn't want Zylan forced into a partnership with her. He wanted more for her. A forced marriage would be hell. She was a being, not an object. Beings had choice.

Chapter Nine

Zylan paced back and forth, his back to the bed that held Neri, who thankfully was out cold. She'd woken once and had had a complete meltdown. Her brain clearly still hadn't processed the rescue. In her mind, she seemed to be still locked in the black room, hanging from the wall, being tortured. It had taken three Slayers to hold her down until the resident doc had pumped her full of enough tranquilizers to take down an elephant.

It killed something inside Zylan, having her scream at his touch, cringing in fear and shielding her face. He wanted to break his fellow Slayer's arms for causing her to scream out in pain. He was willing to kill his friends for doing what they were told, for doing what was needed in order to jab a sleepy-time needle into her arm. He wanted to chase them all away and plant himself in front of her bed with a knife and a gun. He was willing to pump a few rounds into anyone who risked coming back in for her. Love was illogical and unforgiving. He couldn't think straight.

Neri was being assessed by Ester, once a physician. She was an irregular who'd joined the fight when her practice was blown to bits by the Order. She'd been with the Netherworld Agency as a field medic, stitching them up and keeping them alive, for almost as long as Zylan had known Cael. She was their resident doc, and she was damn good at what she did. Sure, she had the bedside manner of a flesh-eating monster, but she cut to the chase and didn't believe in bullshitting anyone.

She was the type to lean over you after a gun fight and say, "Well, it's not good. Your legs have been blown to fuckin' bits and your intestines are being used as a tourniquet. Bad news, you're not gonna live. Good news, because of your intestines, you're not going to bleed out and ruin the carpet."

"She has multiple fractures, broken toes and deep bruising," Ester began, pulling the sheet back over Neri. Pulling her gloves off and tossing them in the trash, she looked to Zylan. "She has suffered a great deal. I'm surprised she's even alive. You can thank your little burden for that." She added that extra dig because he deserved it. "I have viewed Neri's charts from the Netherworld. She's in perfect health. Pregnancy shouldn't be a risk either."

Zylan wanted to puke, his muscles flexed. "Was she raped? Did that sick fuck rape her?"

"There's no evidence of rape or forced entry, which is why I said it shouldn't be a risk. Calm down and listen." Ester had tried to settle him down and failed. It wasn't like she'd tried all that hard either. She had a real problem with the way Zylan had acted toward Amity. Everyone did. He was painfully aware that the doc just didn't bother hiding it like the others did.

Des moved up from the wall she was leaning on. "Zy, breathe. It'll be all right. She's here, she's safe and she has you."

Zylan turned to face Des, anger rippling off him. "How the fuck would you know she's all right? You don't know!"

Des stepped back like he'd hit her.

Cael was beside her in the blink of an eye. "Not cool, Zy. Not cool at all."

Des shook her head and took a deep breath. "I know you're hurting for her, so you get a pass. Do I know how she's feeling? No. I've been in that same room, but still, I have no idea what she's feeling. Trauma is different for all of us. All we can do is be there for her when she wakes up — be there when she can't sleep because the nightmares feel stronger than reality. We can love her. We can support her. We can make damn sure she feels safe here."

"I'm sorry, Des. I wasn't thinking," Zylan whispered, reaching out to her.

Cael stopped his hand. "No, you don't get to hurt her then touch her."

Des smiled, leaning her head into Cael. She looked back to Zylan. "Apology accepted, but don't pull your inner chaos bullshit on me. Use that energy to make things right."

The room cleared out. The Slayers would take shifts, watching over Neri and Amity. Amity had given her first life for Neri. They would do right by her.

* * * *

Lying on the bed, Neri had been semi-aware of her surroundings following her rescue. Before, when the darkness had taken her, alone and cold, she had gone with it, unafraid. Then she could smell Zylan, and she'd vaguely felt him pressed against the outside of her body as she was lost inside it. As she'd staggered blindly within herself, shivering from the cold, she had followed a small stream of warmth.

At first it had rolled over her naked toes, removing the frozen cramps. Slowly the heat had climbed up her legs, drawing her closer toward it. Up ahead was the darkness. As much as she'd wanted to turn and run, she knew she'd be safe tucked inside the hot comfort. She'd known she was running out of time. The darkness had begun growing thicker. She'd struggled to move against it, pushing at it with everything she had.

The temperature had grown hotter and hotter, filling the space until it had become too difficult to breathe. With a loud pop that had knocked her head back and her body to the ground, she'd burned. Screaming through the pain, her body had burst with light, chasing the darkness away.

Her eyes flew open to an unfamiliar room and an unfamiliar face. Her mind remained stuck in survival mode. Her brain tried to remind her that she'd been rescued, but she couldn't grasp it. She rolled sideways, off the hospital bed, and scrambled to the closet corner, screaming.

She didn't remember this room. It was stainless steel, brilliant lights above, trays of hospital equipment, cabinets covering the walls, lino flooring and a set of double doors leading out. Beside the bed, a young man stood, hands in the air, backing up.

"I'm not going to hurt you, Neri," he spoke. His voice was soft and steady, with an attempt at reassurance.

It didn't work. Her eyes darted to the closest silver tray. On top were scalpels. She didn't care if he blocked her. She was going for a blade. She dove for the tray, spilling it onto the floor and grabbing a scalpel. The man did nothing to stop her. He didn't flinch or make a movement.

Neri stood, the coldness of the room making her realize she was standing naked, again.

"What the fuck is it with you people and me being naked?" Neri yelled, lifting her arm to cover her breasts. Her other arm stretched out and was ready to slice the man's throat. There would be no remorse here. She knew half a dozen ways to kill him in no time flat, and she wouldn't hesitate.

The door opened. Sid walked in slowly. "It's over, Nerissa."

She frowned, flashes of memory coming back to her, staggering her. She stared at him. She knew that voice. She remembered thinking she was going insane, hearing voices. She'd chalked it up to psychosis, the beginnings of a padded room of insanity.

"Your voice... I know you," she whispered. "You were there."

Sid nodded. "I was there."

She should have been thankful. Instead, she lunged at him. "You did nothing to help me!"

Sid let her come at him, doing nothing to stop her. He grabbed her wrists to keep her from slicing him up. Sid twisted her back to his chest, still holding her wrists, then pulled her into his body. Wrapping his arms around her, he held her, letting her be angry. She let it all go and he took it. The hate poured out of her.

"I did what I could. I swear to you that I did what I could," he whispered, taking each blow of her hate like a fist to the jaw.

"You didn't help me. Why didn't you help me? I prayed for help," Neri sobbed, sagging against him, the scalpel falling to the floor with a clang.

"I'm sorry, Neri. I suffered with you. I did everything I could think of, including leaving a trail of breadcrumbs to lead Zylan to you. But I could do no more," Sid explained. "I was not allowed."

"I wanted to die." Her soul felt like it had gone ten rounds in a heavyweight boxing championship.

"I couldn't let you. You're not finished yet, Neri," Sid answered. "I couldn't leave you there to die, but I couldn't do anything to help you."

Neri nodded, letting Sid finally pick her up and carry her back to her bed.

"Bane, go get Zy," Sid called out. "Someone she knows needs to be here when she wakes up again, but someone has to stay with Amity. When she wakes up, she'll need help."

"This is so fucked up," Bane said, with a hint of his wolf growling behind his voice. "This isn't going to end well, my friend."

"You're repeating an episode I've already seen, Bane. Now go," Sid barked back. He turned back to Neri. Her eyes were shut, small lines forming from the stress.

Zylan slid into the room, coming to a stop at the bed. "What happened? Bane said she tried to attack you both? What the fuck did you do?"

Sid shook his head, "She woke up. That's what happened. She woke up from being in hell for a week. She's scared, confused and in a lot of pain."

Zylan ran his hand through Neri's hair. His touch made her frown lines fade away and her body shutter into relaxation.

"How's Amity?" Sid asked, giving Zylan another glare.

Sid was still pissed off that Amity had given her life for someone who didn't care about her. But when the going got tough, she'd stepped up to the plate and knocked it out of the park.

"She's holding on," Zylan answered, the weight of his guilt coming out in his words. "I didn't know, Sid."

Sid stepped up to Zylan, pushing his puffed-up chest into Zylan's, glaring, lips twisted into a snarl. "Exactly, Zy. You didn't know. You didn't know because you don't care. I get it. Neri is your Fyrvor, your one true mate. That's fine. That's great. That's just fucking splendid. You treated Amity exactly how you watched your father treat your mother, like an object to be taken out as you please. She was your fucking doormat. But she came through—like she's been bred to do—for you. She gave her fucking life, knowing what it meant, knowing she was saving someone you loved."

Zylan was smart enough to keep his mouth shut.

Sid poked him in the chest. "Amity is dead now, because of you. And all you can do is pity yourself, feel sorry for the shitty life you have. Have you ever thought about her training? Do you know how they trained her to take your abuse? Thirty fucking years of what Neri went through for one week. Thirty years of being abused and kicked. She sees herself in the same light as you see her, worthless and an object. You shouldn't be feeling guilty. You should feel shame. You should feel disgust. That's what I feel when I look at you. I'm fucking *disgusted*."

Sid stepped back then turned his back to Zylan, shaking in anger. He couldn't believe what he'd just said to Zylan, how heavy he'd been. Sid pressed his hand into his chest, his heart pounding. But there was something else.

"Fuck," he growled and walked out. He had feelings for her. *Double fuck*. This wasn't fucking happening.

He took one look back as he closed the doors. Zylan was

sitting beside Neri, running his hand through her hair, as delicately as possible, his cheeks wet from tears. He watched Zylan realize how great Amity's sacrifice had been. The air was thick with regret, sadness and, now, shame.

Sid didn't bother apologizing. Zylan needed a little dose of reality — not the reality that he wanted, but the one that had been hand-delivered and sat on his shoulders. Sid could feel it in his bones. Darkness was coming. No one could run from fate.

* * * *

Zylan stayed at Neri's side, smoothing out her hair. He'd always imagined its softness but never dreamed he'd ever have the chance to touch it. He'd come close once. He'd been making a pit stop at the Netherworld, and she'd been racing toward his elevator, yelling for them to hold it for her. Jumping in and turning around, her ponytail had swung over his face. He could still remember the smell of lilacs and lavender. For weeks after, he'd purchased lilacs and lavender from the local flower shop. The smells helped him sleep, something that did not come easily for him.

Zylan moved from the bed and turned on the radio, finding a classical station. He knew this was her favorite. If she did wake up, he wanted to make sure she could hear something soothing. He knew it didn't matter. She'd be afraid regardless. But just the same, he was driven to ensure her comfort. Turning the music on, it reminded him of each time he'd seen her in the park, light music always following her on her iPod. She'd sit for her hour, eyes closed, face to the sun with her body swaying to the slow beats.

He filled a small metal bowl with warm water and grabbed a white cotton cloth. Placing it on the table beside the bed, Zylan dipped the cloth and began to slowly clean the dried blood from her body. Starting with her delicate hands, he cleaned her skin and soaked her fingernails in the water to remove the crusted memory from her nails. He dried her hands and placed ointment on her cuts.

He brought fresh water with each new body part, meticulously cleaning every square inch of her. He called in Ester to clean her private areas, warning her to be gentle and forgiving. Once Ester was finished and had taken her leave to check on Amity, Zylan went back to Neri, washing her hair and combing it out. From the days of having longer hair, he remembered how to braid it perfectly.

Taking his seat beside her, he stood guard. When she woke up, he wanted to make sure she knew she was safe and that no one here would hurt her. He would do as Des had directed—make her feel safe, acknowledge her fear and support her during her processing of her time spent in hell. It was all he could do.

He felt tiny, insignificant and helpless. His Fyrvor was battered beyond recognition, and there was nothing he could do but love her more. She was a fighter. She was a survivor. Her beating heart was the very reason he was still alive. She was his everything.

Chapter Ten

Anger was a general term for a sudden violent displeasure or a burst of anger. Indignation could also work. It implied deep and justified anger. But those were just the tip of the iceberg, barely touching the emotions Strain was feeling. Rage was vehement anger — rage at being frustrated. Fury was rage so great that it resembled insanity.

Or that was what the dictionary had told him when he'd looked it up. Rage, wrath, insane ravaging hate... Those were a little closer, but not quite. The words barely grazed the surface of what he'd been feeling the moment he'd walked into the compound to find Neri gone and half of his men dead. Okay, his men being dead didn't bother him in the slightest. They'd either died then or they'd be dying now. He was a little pissy that he hadn't had the chance to kill them himself. But just the same, they were dead and deserved it, but he was still ticked off that his men had put themselves in a position to be killed.

Strain took a seat, a drink in his hand, and stared at the bodies on the ground in front of him. Indifferent to their suffering, he was pissed off at the mess more than the loss. He watched as his remaining men cleaned up their failures. He stared at them with hateful and judging eyes. Who would he kill for this? He couldn't blame Garm. He'd been with Strain at his chemical lab. He knew that if Garm had been here, he would have grabbed Neri and left the others to die, just as Strain would have. No sense in losing everything. You pick your battles. If you're not going to win it, save what you can and fuck the rest.

Taking a swig of a drink that sizzled in the pits of his

burning anger, he growled. He couldn't kill the rest of his men. He still needed them. He'd have to punish someone, though. He needed it. He'd drown a puppy at this point. What he wouldn't give for a few whores in this moment. Not only would he penalize them for the actions of others, he'd relieve the buildup that was twitching between his legs.

"They left the other one," Garm spoke up, standing behind Strain.

An ear-to-ear grin slid over Strain's mug. Why would they leave her? They had to have run out of time. They wouldn't have just left someone behind, unless they'd absolutely had to. But he didn't care about the reasons at this point. He'd punish her for tonight. Right now, she was the only one he didn't need. The Slayers knew he had someone else, which meant they'd be coming back...but not tonight. They'd be nursing the sweet Doctor Sung. When they did, he'd be ready.

"Prepare my puppets, Garm. We go out hunting in one hour," Strain called back to his lackey, sucking back the last of his bourbon. He'd get his rocks off before the hunt. He wanted a clear mind. He needed perfect concentration, or he was likely to release his puppets on a pre-school.

The Order had the locations of several members of the upper class — men and women of worth. Fuck this slow and steady bullshit. He'd hit them hard tonight. He'd hit them for what the Slayers had done. He knew his father would have made the same order. Hit them while they were recovering. Cut them off at the knees before they had the chance to regroup.

"You take from me. I take from you," Strain whispered to himself, moving to the farthest room in his compound.

Pushing the door open, his gaze met Sasha's. Strain had taken her weeks ago, keeping her alive as his special little toy. Each time he'd seen his father, he'd punished Sasha. Whenever he was disappointed, she wore that disappointment like a badge. All of his anger, he unleashed on her delicate skin. She was his true puppet, his little toy, his personal amusement that no one else got to play with. No, she was his and his alone. Every boy needed a dog, didn't they? She was his.

"Good evening, Sasha, I see there was a little excitement around here tonight," Strain said, stepping into the room. "They left your ruined body behind. How very sad for you."

Sasha, sitting straight in her wingback chair, smiled. "Good evening, Strain. Indeed, there was quite a bit of commotion tonight. A rather entertaining show, I must admit. I think my favorite part was that they fucked you over. But that's just my opinion. How was your evening, aside from being a complete failure? Your daddy must be proud."

It pissed him off, her pleasant small talk. No matter what he did to her, she smiled. It didn't matter how cruel he'd be, she always remained gracious. If he didn't enjoy her so bloody much, he'd have killed her long ago out of spite. Tonight, he was teetering dangerously close to ending her for the simple reason that he wanted to kill someone. She had no intel. He'd taken her out of interest and because she reminded him of Des — the smell of her body, the texture of her hair, the way her grin said she'd kill you if she could. That reminder was usually why he kicked her.

Sasha was solid muscle and had eyes that made your balls shrivel up and crawl two feet up your asshole. He couldn't figure out what the hell she was, nor would she tell him. She was a brick wall of calm. She didn't panic and never smelled of fear. Never once had she broken a sweat or cried out. She seemed ready every time he came to her. She would brace herself in her bubble of composure and take whatever he dished out. Some days she would speak of his father as if she knew him. Other days, she would speak of Strain as though they'd never met before. At first it was unnerving. Now it was entertaining. She was his amusing toy that he'd never grow bored of.

"What's on the agenda for tonight, Strain?" Sasha asked, standing up and rotating her nude shoulders. He'd once removed her clothing as punishment, but she hadn't cared. Her clothing now lay folded beside the chair, her show of 'go fuck yourself'. "Will we be dancing, as per usual, or have you come up with something a little more interesting? I have grown tired of dancing. I have two left feet."

"Perhaps I'll send Garm in here for the night," Strain countered, smiling right back at her. Only her smile was a little more unsettling than his ever could be in that moment.

He knew she didn't care about any of this. Dead or alive, she was good with either outcome. There truly was nothing he could do to rattle her. And he had tried, right down to dragging innocents to her feet and taking their lives. She didn't blink twice. She would shrug, flick the bloody bits to the floor then go back to picking at her nails or asking for a book to read because she was bored.

Her smile only grew when she saw his. "Fantastic. It's been several days since he and I made love. He is a dash better in bed than you. But don't feel bad, Strain. You could learn. Well, if you'd only take better direction. But that Garm, I tell ya… He knows what a woman wants. He's a fine choice for the night. Thank you."

Strain let his anger push him toward her. Oh, they'd dance tonight. He would waltz her right into submission and eventual unconsciousness. Standing in front of Sasha, he smoothed her hair back, grabbing a fist of it at the base of her neck and jerking her head toward his.

His pain was instantaneous. There was no pause between action and reaction. His brain registered it immediately. Like jumping into a fire, the burn was there before the first flame was seen. When her knee connected with his cock, he doubled over and brought her to the floor with him. Dry heaving, he held her in place.

Her hitting him in the balls was a sure-fire way to ensure her death. The pain radiating from his testicles left him seeing red. To be fair, Strain knew that if the roles had been reversed, he'd have ripped the cock clean off and willingly suffered the death for it.

"Oops. Like I said, I have two left feet," Sasha said, her words rolling into a deafening laughter. Her laughter soon faded, as did she. Strain wrapped his hands around her neck and dragged her into unconsciousness.

Strain stepped out of the room, hating her and respecting her. She had balls, that one. In the face of death, she could laugh. Her bravery wasn't a false one. She was just that fucking tough. A stupid bravery, but brave nonetheless. There would be no dancing tonight. She'd made sure of that. She reminded him of Des, right down to the cocky attitude that would be her death—eventually.

Cursing them both, Sasha and Des, Strain headed out to meet Garm. They had a hunting party to attend, but not before he ordered his men to move Sasha to a new location. He knew the Slayers would return for her, and he wasn't about to make it easy for them. He urged his men to make it snappy. When she came to, she'd beat half of them to death before they could move her. *Spitfire? Yeah, that doesn't cover it—not even close.* She was a wild animal, bloodthirsty, with a killer instinct. *What the fuck is she?*

Putting her out of his mind, he focused on the night. He was looking forward to the party tonight. Strain knew that even if the bitch had disappointed him, Garm wouldn't. His little puppets were lined up in a field and waiting, dead to the world until now. With a wiggle of his pinky finger, they were all his.

Divided up into five teams of five, each given a set of orders, they were off and shambling. Nothing short of a true death brought on by fire would stop them. If there was even the most minute possibility of finding their target, they'd find them and kill them. There would be no bargaining. There would be plenty of begging that wouldn't change the outcome and no answered prayers. Once they were given orders, Strain—and only Strain—could call off the dogs, and he had no plans to do so.

Strain released his monsters into the crystal clear night. Breathing in the fresh air of the forest, he felt alive. He was giddy with anticipation. His hands were shaking with it. He couldn't wait for the carnage to begin. Putting Garm in charge, he headed home. Only his father could wipe this grin off his face.

The Slayers may have taken Nerissa—who would have proven to be useless anyway—but Strain would have the last laugh. He would sleep soundly. Come tomorrow, the fallout from crossing him would be splattered all over the walls of those he'd chosen to die. The power of deciding who would live and who would die tonight was a flavor all of its own. It was better than the sweet intoxication of bringing pain to Des and Cael. This was better than anything he'd ever felt.

Chapter Eleven

Awake, with a clear mind, Neri had Zylan carry her to see Amity. They sat beside the bed, Neri holding Amity's hand. Amity's body was cold to the touch. She was still just as beautiful dead as she probably had been when she was alive. Everything about her, right down to her selfless soul, was beautiful. Amity's touch was familiar. Being near her was familiar. Neri knew it was Amity who had given her life so she could live.

Neri was in rough shape, but she wouldn't remain in her bed when Amity was fighting for her return. Neri wouldn't rest in comfort, knowing that the only reason she was alive was alone in a dark room. She'd forced Zylan to pick her up and carry her to Amity, and she'd been here since. Zylan had reminded her of the risks. When Amity awoke, she'd be starved for blood, and Neri was the perfect little snack. Bane had volunteered to be the first drink, and the rest of the Slayers had followed suit. They had a good supply of blood for Amity. She'd need it. To survive the initial change, she'd need a lot of donors.

Sid sat on the other side of the bed, brushing Amity's hair. "She likes it when her hair looks pretty."

Zylan was curled at Neri's feet, on the floor. "You've got it bad. You've got the loves."

Neri kicked Zylan softly in the chest. "People who live in glass houses shouldn't throw stones."

Zylan grabbed her ankle, pulling it back into his chest. Neri knew he didn't want to let her go. Ever since she'd woken up the previous night, he couldn't be away from her. Each time she'd try to have a moment alone, Zylan would be hit with anxiety attacks. Together, they had spent the day with Amity, checking for signs of her new life.

Neri debriefed with the Slayers, while watching over Amity. She hadn't given up any information to Strain. She was proud of that. Zylan and his men were proud of her for enduring hell to keep her people alive. They had found her banker's box and were in the process of building her a lab for her to continue her work.

"Why don't you two go get some sleep? I'll keep watch," Sid spoke, not looking up from Amity. "This will probably take another day—twelve hours at least. I still can't feel her."

Neri hadn't been tired until Sid mentioned sleep. That one word made her eyelids feel like they were lined with concrete. She blinked lazily, nudging Zylan at her feet.

"Sounds like a good idea. Zy, can I get a lift?"

Zylan stretched out his body, his bones cracking in protest at the movements. "Jeeves, bring the car around."

Neri grinned as Zylan lifted her into his arms. She turned back to Sid. "Sid, please wake me when she wakes up. Swear it."

Sid nodded. Neri and Sid left the room, leaving Sid to meticulously groom Amity for when she woke up. Sid'd told Neri that he'd already polished her nails and given her a pedicure. He'd said he wanted her to feel perfect when she woke. He wanted her to feel pampered for once. She'd had a rough life so far, filled with the kind of training that made a POW camp look like a resort.

Zylan moved toward the infirmary, but Neri shook her head. "Please, I don't want to go back in there. It's a constant reminder of where I was."

"Amity isn't using her bedroom," Zylan said, walking back up the hall.

"Can I stay with you? I don't mean to put you out. I just don't want to be alone. Unless you need to be alone… I don't mean to be presumptuous."

Zylan smiled. "You can stay wherever you feel safe."

Zylan walked to his bedroom, pushing the door open, wishing it looked a little less than a flophouse, bachelor-style. Flipping on the lighting, he saw that his room had been cleaned. There was fresh bedding and candles, with a small sitting area to the right, hosting overstuffed chairs. He knew the chairs. Des had moved them in a few weeks ago, for her and Cael to do morning coffee after their missions. Now they'd been placed into his room. It looked more like a bedroom now and less like a shithole.

He placed Neri on one of the chairs and moved to the bed. A little white card sat at the foot.

You're welcome, dickhead.

Love always, Des and Cael.

P.S. Talk shit to my Fyrvor for a second time, and you'll not wake up again. Des says there are clothes in your closet for Neri.

Zylan grinned, letting out a small laugh. He didn't blame Cael. If anyone so much as touched a hair on Neri's head, he'd fucking kill them.

"This isn't what I expected," Neri said, looking around his clean bedroom.

Zylan ran his hands over his head. "Yeah, it's not what it usually looks like. You can thank Des and Cael."

Neri pointed to the chair beside her. "Are you going to sit or pace?"

Zylan took a seat on his bed. He didn't want to crowd her. He didn't know what to do or how to act. He didn't want to pry, but he didn't want to sit in complete silence either.

Neri slowly stood and started to shuffle over to him. Each step looked as painful as the last.

"What the hell are you doing?" Zylan asked, jumping up and rushing to her side, grabbing onto her arm to balance her.

"I don't want to be alone, Zy. I'm asking for comfort, nothing more. I just... I'm alone...in my head. I want to fill my own silence with something, anything," Neri whispered, moving to the bed, Zylan in tow.

He helped her onto the bed and under the blankets. He

climbed over her and lay down beside her. He froze when she rolled into him, placing her head on his chest.

"Tell me a story—any story, funny or sad. Something, please," she asked.

He found himself whispering while running his hand through her hair. At first, he felt uncomfortable, like touching her was wrong. Soon, she was laughing with him, as he told her stories of his first bombed kiss, fighting with his siblings and his first hunt that had ended with him catching a bird and it trying to peck his eyes out. Once his body relaxed against hers, it felt natural. It felt right. He felt like no one could touch them in this moment. Regardless of his path, he would always have this moment.

"Since my father died, I don't think I've ever felt this safe," Neri said, her voice sounding groggy.

Neri rolled her body tighter into Zylan's arms. Zylan knew nothing could touch her here. Nothing could hurt her. He would see to it. She had a warrior who would fight to his death for her.

When she stopped talking and her breathing deepened, he stayed with his arms wrapped tightly around her, his breathing matching hers. It was the deepest he'd ever slept. For ten years he'd always been on guard, ready to run from a fate that was nipping at his ass like hunting dogs.

It had felt like they'd just closed their eyes when Bane charged into the room, holding his bloodied neck. "Holy shit, she's awake."

Neri jerked, sitting straight up then trying to crawl out from under the covers. Zylan jumped up then lifted her into his arms. He couldn't bear to watch her struggle on her broken and taped-up toes. With her in his arms, they flew down the hall, yelling at everyone to get out of their way.

Cael stepped in front of the door, holding his hand out. "Give her a moment. She's just coming around now."

"Cael, respectfully, get the fuck out of our way." Zylan's words were harsh and heated.

Cael shrugged and stepped to the side. "If she eats you,

don't come crying to me."

Amity stood in the corner, drenched in blood, her eyes darting around the room. She looked scared, caged and starved.

"Put me down, and go to her," Neri whispered. "Please, help her."

Zylan put Neri down in a chair by the door, motioning for someone to stand beside her, in case Amity let loose.

With his hands up, he moved toward Amity. "Amity, it's okay. It's me, Zylan."

Her eyes flickered from Zylan to Neri. Her lips curled her face into twisted anger. She stepped forward, hissing at Neri. Zylan stepped into Amity's line of sight, removing Neri from her vision. Vampyres by nature were highly territorial. That's all he needed, a fight that ended with him having to kill Amity to protect Neri.

Zylan did the only thing he knew how to do—made himself the target, put himself in harm's way to protect innocents. It was all he knew. He moved toward Amity, grabbing her arms and spinning her around, pulling her back into his chest with her arms crisscrossed against hers.

This reminded him of watching cowboys on bucking broncos. She thrashed in his arms, trying to get away. He'd seen this happen many times. It took time to come back, time to remember who you were. He would hold on to her for all time, if that's what it took. It was that or have to put her down, which he'd seen happen as well, when they didn't come back from the other side, stuck in a state of feral animal. Those unfortunates were revenants, zombies and bloodthirsty with no higher brain power.

Sid joined Zylan, standing in front of Amity. He cracked his neck. "Zy, you'd better be holding on damn hard. I'm about to hotwire her memory."

"Shit, you can do that?"

"It's not going to be a walk in the park. It's gonna hurt something fierce," Sid said and grabbed onto Amity.

Holding on to her, Zylan touched the edge of the pain,

just a taste of what Amity was feeling. She bucked like she'd been electrocuted. Her entire body pitched off the floor. Both he and Sid held on, while Amity screamed one hell of a scream. Their ears would ring for weeks.

On the edge of Amity's memories, he saw glimpses of Sid's memories with Neri. Flashes slammed into Zylan's brain—moments between Sid and Neri, Sid holding onto Neri's hand as she had been tortured, Sid begging for help, begging the Orygin for aid. Sid had been given a choice—intervene and Neri would die as a result or be at her side and she would live. Sid had wanted to intervene, but his love for Zylan had kept him in the shadows. Each time Strain had come to Neri, Sid had stood at her side and pulled as much pain from her as he could, while maintaining the shadows that cloaked him.

With regret he could hardly bear now, Zylan remembered that each brutal time Sid had returned to the compound, filled with pain and hurt, he'd been met by Zylan and his hate. Sid jerked, shutting down his own memories, then let go and staggered backward. Amity and Zylan fell to the floor. Zylan and Sid kept eye contact momentarily, just long enough for Zylan to know exactly what Sid had endured for the Slayers. One nod was all it took, and both men had an understanding. Zylan would never question Sid again, and he wouldn't allow anyone else to either.

Amity, no longer in Zylan's grip, rolled away and jumped to her feet. She moved around Sid, ducked under Cael, shoved Bane to his back and slid on the floor to a stop in front of Neri.

Neri didn't flinch. "Amity?"

Amity blinked. "I knew you'd make it." Neri reached out to Amity, who backed up. "Not yet. I can hear the blood pumping through your veins. I can smell your body, just beneath your skin. I do not trust myself to touch you yet."

Zylan had moved, putting himself between them. "Move back, Amity."

Amity ducked her head. "As you wish, sire."

"Wait, Amity? Are you with us?" Zylan asked, feeling like he'd just kicked the one person he owed his world to.

She nodded, her eyes on the ground.

Zylan grabbed her, making her flinch, then he pulled her into his arms. "Thank you. Thank you, Amity. Thank you."

Her body slowly relaxed. "Sire, I cannot breathe."

With a laugh, he released her back into Sid's arms. He hugged her just as tightly.

"All that work to pretty you up, and you're covered in blood." Sid laughed.

Neri had Zylan help her to her feet. "Thank you, Amity, for all you have given. I cannot ever repay you."

Amity took a shaking breath. "Love him. Love him as he loves you, and that is payment enough. I will find a way to undo this."

Zylan and Neri didn't hang around for the remaining feeding. This was usually a private matter for a Vampyre. Sid would remain to make sure everyone made it out alive. Neri and Zylan would sleep — together, soundly and safely.

Zylan carried Neri back to his bedroom, breathing her in, trying to hold her scent inside long enough to stain his lungs with her. Tucking Neri back into bed, he would live the dream tonight. Come tomorrow, reality would set in. Regardless of what Amity had said, there was no way to undo this. There was no way around it. He would have to return to Sola-Nosfer. He would be killed during his Reaping, then he'd be forced to marry Amity and rule over their people. The idea of leaving Neri was a pain too great to dwell on tonight. He wouldn't hate Amity. In the end, he would treat her well and with honor. She had earned it and more. He would give her unprecedented freedom and love, but it would not be true love. It would be the kind of love you gave someone you respected.

Tonight he'd hold onto Neri, because tonight it was just them. *Fuck the rest.* He pulled Neri closer. He felt uneasy, like the calm before a coming storm. That's exactly what this was. She was the calm, and his future was the brewing storm.

Chapter Twelve

"I've never smelled anything so beautiful," Amity whispered, twirling in the hallway, holding her gauze gown out at either side.

Sid leaned against the wall with one foot up, watching her hair twist and float in the air as she twirled. The smell she was referring to was Zylan and Neri and their love. Amity, a full Vampyre for a week now, had wandered the compound, sniffing the air with Bane. With each new smell, Bane would give it a name. Her favorite, by far, was the smell of love.

Everyone had been woken up because of her following her nose and ending up on top of them in their sleep, her face pressed to their hair. No one minded. They were used to odd around these parts. Not even Zylan or Neri minded. Their love for each other had extended to Amity.

"Sidriel," Amity sang out from deeper down the hall.

"Why can't you call me Sid, like everyone else does?" Sid called back.

Her giggle echoed against the walls. "Sidriel is your name, is it not?"

She flowed out of the hall, more graceful than ever before. Amity didn't just move. She glided, the way sunbeams shone down through thick forest. She had gained perfect control of her Vampyre side within a few hours of waking. Part of that was due to her perfect breeding and training, and part of it was because of who she was, the real Amity. Over this past week, she had grown with her freedom. Twice, during dinner, she had turned down different foods. Why? Because she'd said they tasted like *shit*. Everyone blamed Sid for her new-found vocabulary and behavior. Amity didn't. She thanked him every day.

Amity had grown close to Neri. A piece of her soul, after all, was tucked inside Neri for all time. More than that, Amity understood why Zylan loved Neri more than life and death. Neri was beautiful and smart, brave and fearless. She was a warrior in her own way. She fought with her mind and her soul.

Amity had grown close to everyone at the compound. She spent time with Riam — origin unknown to everyone — who was a pillar of calm and had a love so powerful deep inside him for each and every comrade there. Each death of an innocent he'd said felt like a bullet to the head, Amity agreed. Amity knew that Riam was what most men could only aspire to become.

Bane had taken Amity under his sniffer wing. He'd spent countless hours with her, keeping her safe, but teaching her how to use all of her senses to her advantage. Teaching her how to smell a lie, how to smell weakness, but, more importantly, how to smell danger. He'd taught her to trust the prickles of gooseflesh that would cover her at the oddest of times. He'd taught her how to be on constant alert in the back of her mind, while enjoying the smaller pleasures of life. Bane had taught her how to be a wolf in sheep's clothing. Amity said she loved his laughter most, loved how it would fill up his eyes and burst out in liquid joy.

Amity loved spending time with Desdemona Bloodworth, orphan, Prophetyc and, in Des' words, a half-breed. She was everything Sidriel had told Amity she was, but more. Amity could see the future in her eyes. She could see hope, and Amity felt solid around her. Des — as she preferred to be called — grounded everyone. She sheltered all from a storm, taking it all and protecting those who couldn't fight. Knowing Des gave Amity a backbone. She'd watched Des go toe to toe with each man here, and never once would she back down. She had an opinion, and death was the only thing that could keep that opinion safely inside her. But

Amity saw that the part every Slayer loved most about Des was the fire that burned inside her for Cael.

Meeting Cael had been a special treat for her. She'd never met a man like him before. She saw parts of him that inspired her. He wasn't as friendly as the rest. It wasn't because he didn't care. It was because he cared so much. He was usually lost in his own world of constant worry. The only silence he received was when Des was touching him. She grounded him and focused him. He clung to her like a life raft. Cael was fearless, protective and thought of himself as the Aegys for them all, their protector. He would sooner die than fail them. Amity found strength in Cael, and she watched him speak as though he was a god. She nodded and would take notes, wanting to learn from the man who would die for people he didn't even know.

Then there was Sidriel — Sid to his friends. Amity called him by his whole name, only because she enjoyed his wrinkled brow and frown. Sidriel was stuck between doing what was right overall and doing what was right in that very moment. He wanted to save everyone but wasn't allowed. He wanted to jump in head first, without looking. Amity knew that his heart was in constant pain, pain for those he failed and those he knew he'd fail. He could see farther down the road than anyone here, including Riam. He would trade his life for any one of them, but he didn't have a life to trade. His life was not his to barter with. He existed. He didn't live. Amity spent each day reminding him that he was not an object. He was a being with choice, as he'd once told her — only his choices were shaped by fate, not destiny.

"Sidriel, can we go out dancing?" Amity called down the hall, still twirling and breathing in the smells that hung in the air. "I listened to Desdemona and one of your new recruits, Able, speaking of a dancing house downtown."

"A club? You want to go to a club?" Sid asked, stepping away from the wall.

Amity poked her head out of the darkness of the hall and

nodded.

"I want to celebrate my death. I was not granted a Reaping. There has been no celebration," Amity said, her eyes almost begging him. "Please, Sidriel—just one hour."

"You will need to change. I'll have to round up a few Slayers," he agreed.

"Slayers? That is not a celebration. That is a hunt. I do not wish to go on a hunt, although Bane has stated I would make an excellent Slayer," Amity said, planting her feet firmly and staring Sidriel in the eyes.

"They don't have to be with us, but I can't take you down there alone. I won't risk it. We either have a few Slayers spread out, just in case, or it's a no go."

Amity wrinkled her nose then nodded. "Deal."

Sidriel shook his head. "You're going to be the death of me."

"You can't die, so don't pout." Amity giggled and tore off running back into the darkness of the hall. "Desdemona! I need clothes. Sidriel is taking me to a dancing house… A club. He's taking me to celebrate."

* * * *

Wearing skintight black leather pants, a black sparkly backless shirt that tied around her neck with one strap around her shoulders, black boots just under her knees with a small heel, her hair pulled into a tight ponytail and a dash of makeup, she met Sidriel in the front room. She knew she'd aced all ten steps by the look on his face.

Zylan met her first, giving her a small box. He told her that it was a gift he'd picked up a few days before. It was meant to be given when they returned to Sola-Nosfer. Smiling, she opened the box. Inside, a small bracelet, a little charm with three hearts hung off of it. Her hands shook as she lifted it from the box.

"I will treasure this for all time, sire. Thank you," Amity whispered, allowing Zylan to place it around her wrist.

"It's from both Neri and me. No matter the outcome, we will always be grateful for the time you have given us," Zylan said, placing a small kiss on her forehead. "And please, stop calling me sire. I am Zy to you, always."

Neri stepped forward, clutching Amity's hands. "I will forever love and cherish you. You are with me forever."

Bane gave her a small charm to add to her bracelet. "It is engraved with the marking of my people. If ever you are in trouble, you may give this charm, and you will be taken to my people. Show them this, and they will find me. I will find you, always."

Ester, the resident doc, stepped forward with her own charm. "This is a symbol of strength. When you are at your weakest, I give you my strength to see you through the darkness."

As each person stepped forward, her charm bracelet filled up with little tokens of how much they really cared for her. She was left speechless. She hadn't realized that so many of them truly saw her or cared so much for the woman whom fate had decreed would take one of their men from them.

Riam stepped up and took a moment, looking her in the eyes. She could feel the weight of his stare pushing on her soul. He placed a small charm on her bracelet, a small flashlight. "To help you find your way back from the darkness, always."

Sidriel was last. One solid heart, placed on her bracelet, had meant more than the rest. They both stepped outside and were off into the night. Sid would drive and six others would be set up around the club. He wouldn't bring her to Blood Alley, even though the clubs were the best the city had to offer. It was far too dangerous for her there.

She spent the trip excited. No one had guessed she had a plan beyond dancing. It took an hour to drive there, and she filled the time with talking about little things she'd never noticed before. She wasn't trained to talk about things unless it was of interest to her mate. But tonight, she filled the air with topics that made Sid smile and laugh.

"We're almost there," Sid called out to her.

She turned her face to him, her smile ear-to-ear. Her excitement added to his. He now looked just as eager as she felt. A first for her, and, in a way, she knew this was a first for him.

They parked and walked up the sidewalk, around the long line of partygoers. Sid gave his name at the door. A man dressed in black gave a nod and lifted a red rope. The doors opened, and they were both hit with heat and the sound of bass. Sid pulled her in behind him. They checked their coats and headed straight for the dance floor.

The songs changed, bleeding from one to the next, Amity not missing a beat. Song after song, she danced. Finally coming to a stop, she touched her throat, signaling thirst. Sid pointed toward the bar and grabbed her hand, pulling her back out of the sweating and pulsating crowd.

He grabbed two bottles of water, and they moved over to a small table on the edge of the dance floor.

"That was amazing," Amity yelled over the music.

Sid pointed to his watch. She didn't want to end the night, but she knew she shouldn't keep Slayers from the field.

Amity leaned in, still smiling. "Thank you, Sidriel. This has been the best night of my life."

Sid nodded in agreement. "This has been one of the best nights of my existence. I don't want it to end, but we must go."

"I need to go to the Ladies room before we depart," Amity said. It was time for her ultimate plan.

Sid pointed to the back, to a door with a white figure in a dress. Following her to the bathroom, he waited against the wall, while Amity stepped inside.

The bathroom was like every other bathroom she had seen on television and in books. Or magazines, as Des had called them. It smelled worse than she had thought it would. She could smell urine and vomit, sweat and what Bane would have called desperation. She scanned the room, finding small windows lining the top of the ceiling, against the back. Tucking herself into the stall, she climbed up and unlatched the window.

She knew where the other Slayers were. They wouldn't see her climbing out and into the alley below. Pulling herself up and out, she dropped then rolled on the ground below, skinning her elbows. Her heart pounded with her decisions, but they were hers to make.

She ventured farther down into the alley, letting her sense of smell guide her. At the end of the alley, to the right, she found him—a complete stranger who smelled of regret and anger. He leaned against a wall, a needle hanging out of his arm. He pumped in the rest of his poison and pulled the needle out, tossing it to the ground.

He stepped forward. "You've taken a wrong turn somewhere, blondie."

It took her two tries, but she finally spoke, stepping closer to him. "No wrong turns."

His lips parted in a smile, exposing rotting teeth. "What can I do for you, pretty lady?"

Amity pulled the top button loose on her pants, trying for a sultry grin, the kind she had seen in the movies.

The man filled with poison stepped forward, pulling his jeans open. "I think I can help you out there."

"No, you can't," Sidriel spoke, stepping down the alley.

"Mind your business, mister," the druggie spoke up, glaring toward the voice. The sound of a gun clicking changed his mind. He pulled his pants closed and stepped away. "I'm good. I'm gone. I don't need this shit."

Sidriel stepped up to Amity with her coat on his arm as the druggie ran off down the alley, back to safety. "What the hell do you think you're doing?"

Amity grabbed her jacket and pulled it on, ashamed but angry. "You have no right to intervene, Sidriel. As you said yourself, it is my life, my choice."

"Give me a good goddamn reason why you were about to fuck some disease-infested crackhead, and I'll go drag him back here for you. Hell, I'll keep your six until you're done.

But the reason better be life or fucking death, Amity. Any other reason isn't good enough."

Amity looked back at Sid, her cheeks flushed from embarrassment. "To save Zylan and Neri. If I am tarnished, he will not be forced to marry me. If I am ruined, he will not have to leave his Fyrvor. So yes, it is life or fucking death, Sidriel. To me, it is."

Her words started strong and angry, only to end as a whisper, filled with shame. She would take it — and more — to save Zylan and Neri, to keep their love alive. She would carry that shame with her for all time, for them.

"You know how you want to do something to save someone, but you're stopped each time? That's how I feel in this moment. You took away my choice to do what I could do. I have limited options, Sidriel, and you just took away the only one I had. Why? Why would you do that?"

Sid pulled her into his arms, walking her back out of the alley. "I will help you, Amity, but not like this — never like this. You cannot give yourself to someone who doesn't care about your life or your love."

He helped her into the car and climbed in, driving back in complete silence. She knew that he could identify with how she was feeling in this moment. To try to do something to help someone, only to be blocked in the end — to be willing to sacrifice yourself for someone else, only to be stopped when you've come so close. Amity knew Sidriel had been in her shoes, maybe not in some dank back alley, but he'd hit the same level of desperation.

He opened the door for Amity, holding out his hand for her. He watched her try to collect herself before stepping out. She was always a model of perfect breeding, never showing weakness or emotion. "I *will* help you, Amity."

"The only way you can help me is to ruin me for him, and he will hate you for it," Amity answered.

"I know. But don't worry about me. They've all hated me at one time or another. And I'm sure they'll hate me again for some other reason."

Amity gripped his hand tighter. "Swear to me, on your honor, that you will help me."

Sid swallowed and gave his word. Amity jumped into his arms, wrapping hers around his neck, kissing his cheek.

"Thank you, Sidriel. Thank you," she said, over and over. Her smile was back to its usual delight. With a bounce in her step, she led them back into the house.

Most of the Slayers were gone out on hunts. Zylan was with Neri in her lab. Amity could hear her laughter carry down the halls. Des and Cael were out on separate hunts, but soon the house would fill with the sound of them reuniting.

Amity didn't waste time. She pulled him straight to his bedroom, a place where they had both spent a lot of time together, usually lying on the floor, talking about things she didn't understand and him doing his best to explain them, usually without success.

Amity stripped out of her clothing and placed herself face up on the bed. She closed her eyes and steadied her breathing. She was schooled in the art of lovemaking. She knew this would hurt. She'd been told that sex would probably hurt every time her mate came to her hips.

Sidriel dropped his clothes on the floor and climbed onto the bed beside her, placing his hand on her stomach. "Open your eyes, Amity. Please. I can't do this — not like this, not when all I can smell is your fear."

Amity opened her eyes, turning her head to Sid. "Please, Sid, please just do it. I'm sorry. I'm sorry this will not be what you are accustomed to, but I beg of you, just do it."

Sid climbed on top of her, putting himself between her thighs. He rested his elbows under her shoulders, holding her face.

"You're beautiful, Amity. You deserve the stars and moon," Sid whispered, rubbing his thumbs over her cheeks. He whispered little bits of sweetness until she opened her eyes again.

Amity finally smiled. "Thank you, Sid."

She slowly lifted her head, placing her lips against his, not because she had seen this done by others or on television, but because she wanted nothing more than to kiss him. Sid lowered his hand and prepared her as best he could. With one slow movement, he pushed himself into her, eating her whimpers with his mouth.

Her fate was sealed with a kiss.

Both of them sealed their destinies in that moment.

* * * *

Zylan looked up from the floor, sitting at Neri's feet as she worked at her laptop. He rubbed his sternum, feeling the same pressure he'd felt before. Chalking it up to exhaustion, he stood, lifting his Fyrvor into his arms. She didn't fight him. At one time, he knew that she would have fought tooth and nail to remain working—but not with Zylan, not ever with him.

He carried her back to his room—their room—placing her gently on the bedding. He retrieved her night clothes and turned his back, giving her privacy. Neri had said she thought he was being silly, but Zylan couldn't help it. He waited for her to dress then he tucked her into bed, crawling in beside her, his boxer shorts still on. The thought of being nude with her made his stomach flop. She deserved more than that. After what she'd been through, he wouldn't dare make her endure something that made her feel even the slightest bit of discomfort. He was there to keep her safe, not press his nudity onto her.

Spooning her, the pressure in his chest released. Being close to Neri did that for him. His worries would leave just as soon as they would settle.

"What's wrong, Zy?" Neri whispered into the dark.

"I don't know. Something felt *off*, but it's gone now," Zylan responded, pulling her tighter.

"Look into it tomorrow. Don't ignore it. I've heard a few people say the same thing these past few days."

With a nod, Zylan let it go for the night. He knew something was wrong, but couldn't put his finger on it. He'd mentioned it to Riam, who'd said nothing, as if he'd say anything at all. The sky could be falling around him, and Riam wouldn't have mentioned it. Sid? Well, that was a lost cause. Sid spoke in riddles, if at all.

Zylan drifted off.

Chapter Thirteen

The sound of flesh on flesh was the round of applause Strain needed. Fucking always felt like a pat on the back. His hips pounded harder and faster into a new worker at The Hemlock, slapping against her milky flesh. She, like hundreds before her, was brand new to the scene. He could tell she was new. Aside from the lack of scabbed-over needle marks, she didn't feel like sinking his prick into a warm bowl of gravy. Her body grabbed onto his with each stroke. Soon, if she lived long enough, she would feel like the others had—a bottomless pit of regret and hordes of past johns.

His balls tightened, his first warning of what was yet to come. He pulled from the whore and pushed her to her knees. She swallowed him down her throat with skill. He didn't bother looking at her. He already knew what he'd see. Regret. Anguish. Remorse. Her eyes would be bloodshot, and she would have a runny nose from crying. *The usual.* They all were contrite, with bad decisions and too many dead ends.

He pulled himself from her mouth and tucked his cock back into his pants. He did the usual dance, tossing bills onto the floor with a small baggie of H, laced with chemical. She picked up the bills and left the drugs on the floor. Stepping around him, shaking her head, she left the room. He listened to her close the door in the bathroom beside him. He listened to her place a phone call and talk to four different kids, reminding them that it was past their bedtime.

He opened the door of his bathroom, and he stepped out,

refreshed. He stopped at her bathroom and pushed the door open. She stood, shocked and embarrassed, cleaning the streaming tears from her face.

"Why? If you feel like a filthy whore after, why do it?" Strain asked, more out of curiosity than any other reason.

She shrugged. "I work. I work damn hard, but it isn't enough. It's never fucking enough."

"Where are their fathers?"

She glared. "Typical, asshole. There was only one father. He's dead, and no, it wasn't drug related or gang shit. He was a good man and provided for his family. He was in the wrong place at the wrong time. The typical shit story the cops tell every widow."

"Why did you leave the smack on the floor? You could have at least sold it for a few extra bucks," Strain asked, leaning against the door.

"Listen. I'm a whore, not an addict. I sell my soul to put food on my table for my kids and to pay for a roof over their heads. Don't you stand there and fucking judge me. You just paid to fuck me. What does that say about you?" she snapped back, defending her need to reduce herself to a piece of dirty meat.

Strain couldn't believe he was doing this. He pulled out his wallet and unloaded every dime onto the counter. Then he put down his unlimited credit card.

"Pack your shit and go home," he said, pushing the pile of money toward her.

"I don't need your pity. I've made it this far without anyone," she whispered, new tears rolling down her cheeks.

"This isn't free money, little girl. You'll earn it."

She shook her head. "I'm not going to be your on-call fuck toy. Sorry. I don't work like that. I come in when I need the money. I won't be owned or pimped out."

Strain nodded. "Not as ass. This club is mine in two weeks. I will need a manager or bookkeeper or someone. I'm offering you a job—one that'll pay your bills then some."

She lifted her head, her mouth open in pause. "An honest job? No more sex?"

"None. At least you won't be the one on your back. I need someone who knows the biz, knows the routine and is clean and sober. It's your choice. Take the card. Think of it as an expense account. Get your bills in order, pay off your debts. You can call it your signing bonus."

"You need a pimp, then. That's what you're asking me to do?" she asked, her voice still angry.

He didn't bother bullshitting her. "Similar, but not quite. Sex work is the oldest profession in the book. I've decided we'll give them a place to work, safely. There will be no drugs, no booze and no more abuse. I'm not offering to save anyone. I'm offering to keep them alive while they do what they're going to do out in the dank alleys."

She nodded slowly, finally agreeing and extending her hand. "Deal."

"I'll have your paperwork delivered. Keep your ass out of here unless it's to work for me. No drugs. That's an absolute."

She grabbed some brown paper towel and started writing her name and address. Strain shook his head.

"I know who you are, Prudence," Strain said and stepped out of the bathroom.

The small part of him that still held onto a hair-sized strand of humanity was proud of what he'd just done. The larger part of him that bathed in the pools of evil didn't do anything without a selfish reason. He knew that although he'd done her a solid, he was going to use her in the end. His self-interest always outweighed his charity, because nothing in this world was free. Whether it was out of kindness or madness, it all came at a price. And at the end of the day, the books always balanced.

Strain was buying up Blood Alley, and he needed the humans as a front. He needed to squirm his way back into mankind without raising suspicions. Time and time again, he was seen down here when all of the worst crimes were taking place. He knew that eventually, his being seen would land him behind bars. He needed to start creating sound alibis. Owning half the city block would be a solid reason. Plus, having a constant bank roll and a 'Plan B' would help his little side projects. This would also keep Garm from getting restless. He would be partial owner, and Strain would stay as a silent partner.

He always had a 'Plan B'. He'd learned long ago to always have something to fall back on. If shit were to hit the fan, he wasn't about to let himself freeze, out in the cold.

Strain took his usual seat, mentally redesigning the club. This would be the hottest place in Van City by the time he was done. The server stopped off with a fresh drink and went about her business, which included cleaning the bathroom he was just in.

Prudence finally emerged, the makeup cleaned from her face, her hair pulled back in a bun and her shirt buttoned up to the collar. She'd left the shit life behind in that bathroom, flushing it down the toilet, along with her regret. The fact that she'd left the smack on the floor had made him offer her a way out. Finding someone in this business who wasn't high as fuck was harder than finding a clean cop around here.

He knew his server would find the smack on the floor and, like the fool she was, she'd pocket it. Regardless of her brain power, she was a good hostess. Sadly, tonight would be her last night. She'd suck that shit up her nose or drop it deep within a vein then be down for the count. He'd consider this her notice. He'd miss her coked-out smile and bouncy tits.

Garm took a seat in front of him. "Sir, the job is complete."

Strain smiled and breathed in a breath of victory. It was a small victory, but a win just the same. Garm gave only the details he knew Strain would be interested in and didn't bother with the filler.

According to Garm's report, all five families Strain had ordered hits on had been slaughtered in their beds. No one had been spared. It had been a bloody mess. Bits and pieces had littered the floors of each bedroom. It was a message to the Netherworld. Strain had the power, not them. *Cross me again, and it will only get worse.* Tonight could have been a complete destruction of their think tank, those who made the decisions. Tonight Strain could have cleaned house. This would be their only warning.

He toasted the air, sending Garm on his way, but not before informing Garm that he would own a small portion of The Hemlock. Garm was pleased. It was more responsibility and was the promotion Garm had been itching for. Garm took his leave, as directed, taking a look around the club on his way out.

Tonight Strain wanted to be alone. He wanted to revel in his own madness. He wanted to wrap himself up in his hate and drink to it. The Slayers had brought this on themselves. *There's no running from fate and no hiding from the darkness.*

Strain would begin phase two. Wound by wound, he would bring the Slayers to their knees, begging for mercy. But they would find no mercy with him.

Chapter Fourteen

"For fuck's sake, Zy!"

Des' voice could barely be heard over the thunder of Zylan's bike coming to a dead break against a tree. The face-first stop didn't slow Zylan down. If anything, it gave him extra momentum. Zylan jumped from his bike just as it touched down, leaping free and landing in a full-out run.

Des punched the gas, trying to catch up. It was like chasing a tornado. Zylan zigzagged down the hill on the ankles of two members of the Order. They weren't their targets for the night, but Zylan didn't seem to care. He killed anything that even hinted at being a part of Neri's interrogation. He was a man on a mission, and all Des could do was catch up and watch. There would be no stopping him tonight—or any other night.

Des didn't let Zylan out of her sight, as she pulled to a complete stop, her bike not kissing bark like his did. Des climbed off, pulling out her trusted nine-millimeter. It fit perfectly in her hand, light enough to run with without tiring your wrists or grip. Then again, a Slayer would have lugged a bazooka around if it was their best option. Holding her gun and sidestepping into the field, she listened to the forest. She was on Zylan's six, keeping lookout for backup. Proletaryans traveled in packs like ravenous dogs, minus the higher brain power.

In the middle of the field, Zylan was throwing down with two of the Order's largest men. The Slayers had noticed, over time, that Strain wasn't hiring string beans. His followers were getting bigger and bigger, with skilled training in hand-to-hand combat. *Great, Strain is hiring from the MMA pool.*

Des wouldn't bother taking a shot at one of the SOBs. She knew better than that. If she took one down, Zylan would rage. It had to be him and only him. He had to avenge his Fyrvor. He had to be the one to restore her honor. She'd made the mistake of taking down a member of the Order before Zylan could throttle them—once and never again. Zylan had lost his shit on her. Now she'd hang back and make sure no creepy crawlies came out of the woodwork. If they did, she still wouldn't intervene. She'd whistle a heads-up to Zylan.

The Slayers were all out in the field now, everyone taking rotations. Strain had sent his monsters to the front doors of agents, the decision-makers, the policy writers. Strain had not just hit agents. He'd taken out their entire families.

Two nights ago, Captain Salas Warner had shown up at the compound of the Slayers. Showing up on their doorstep, unannounced, had almost ended with him being shot in the head. If it hadn't been for Bane smelling Warner, he'd have been taken out five kilometers down the road.

Warner had given them the news. Five of the most influential families of the Netherworld had been slaughtered in their homes. Security footage showed Proletaryans. They were in and out in less than five minutes. By the time the police could respond to the alarm systems going off, every member of the household was gone. The scene was unlike anything that'd ever seen. It was cruder in some way. The carpets were soaked with blood and body parts. This was a message from Strain. He was more evil than the Slayers were willing to be.

Orders had come down from the top brass. The Netherworld wanted the Slayers to step it up. Cael had lost his shit. They all *had* stepped it up long ago. Each member had been working in shifts with no rotation breaks. But Warner had made it clear—recruitment would take priority. Once the Slayers' ranks had been built up, they were to wipe out the Order. Mass extermination by whatever means possible. Anything else was secondary.

Des slowly made her way down the hill, step by step, toward Zylan. From the right, two men from the Order emerged. Des gave two short bursts of a whistle, notifying Zylan that two more were about to be on his ass. Des picked up her pace a little, lifting her gun and keeping them in her line of sight. If either of them lifted a weapon, she'd put a bullet between their eyes. Des was nothing more than a glorified babysitter of a man who was on the verge of a complete meltdown. Zylan was on the razor's edge of insanity.

Little droplets of water fell from the sky. Van City was known as the pit stop for every single rain cloud in the world. If it wasn't raining, it was too hot to breathe. She knew Zylan preferred the rain. Mixed in the scent of leaves and pine, Des could smell the broken-down bike and blood. The stench of death was only going to get worse with Zylan on his rampage.

Zylan caught Des moving out of the corner of his eye. She'd found a stump ten meters back from the hand-to-hand fight and had taken a seat. The two who'd joined the fight were now gagging on their egos. They'd been dumb enough to jump in without a single weapon. Zylan had beaten them both to a pulp. He'd hit them over and over, and, at one point, he'd used one of them to beat the other. Zylan was sure it was a sight to see but not a show that Des enjoyed.

Zylan stared down at his own version of war. It had taken him six and a half minutes from the time the nose of his bike had kissed the juicy bark of the tree to now, with all four dead at his feet. This included robbing them of their phones, weapons and wallets. Any intel they could get, they took. The extra weapons helped, too. Killing them with their own guns was the icing on the cake. It wasn't until he had unloaded their gear that he finally stopped and took a breather. His stomach growled, but it wasn't out of hunger. It felt as if he'd just finished a pie-eating contest, and he was the winner.

Looking at the mess of bodies, bloodied and bruised, broken and lying at odd angles, his stomach heaved. In the moment, he couldn't stop himself. He couldn't hold back, even when he tried. A driving force pushing him forward. He had to avenge his Neri. He had to hunt down each and every one of them to punish them for what they'd done to her. He wouldn't stop until his fingers were wrapped around the Strain's throat.

Des stood to his back, shaking her head. Her gun out, she moved forward. "You make my job ten times harder, Zy. I have to touch them after you've tortured them. Thanks for that."

Zylan stepped back, making room for her. "They deserved it—and more."

"I'm sure they did, but I don't. Get the fuck away from me while I do this," Des snapped, kneeling down and pulling off her glove.

She knelt down over a man whose face was hamburger. Not even dental records would help to identify who he'd once been. Fingerprints could have worked, but they were about to torch the bodies. Zylan stood nearby as she ran her hand over the beaten man's arm. She didn't touch him completely. Riam and Sid were teaching her how to use her abilities and not allow her abilities to use her. Zylan watched her process. She would think of what she wanted to see, then would graze them with her touch.

She would be hit with flashes of what had just taken place, the fear and pain and likely a wish that it would finally end and that Zylan would just kill him. From there, she would be given the answers they needed. Tonight, the only question the Slayers wanted to know was the location of the other Proletaryans.

She stood then, still glaring at Zylan. "All he knows is that they are being held in a storage bunker, out near the airport maybe. I couldn't see where—only what it looks like from the inside. It's made completely of concrete—floors, walls and ceiling—piping running above, drains on the floors. I could hear what I think are airplanes, a helicopter maybe."

Zylan called in to Cael, giving him the new intel, then hanging up while Cael was in mid-sentence. "We're being called home."

Des turned away while Zylan lit up his most recent shit-storm, torching the bodies at his feet. Maybe if it had been someone else, Des wouldn't have been able to stomach it, but he and Des were close. They were paired together in the field and had shared some serious close calls. Zylan wasn't a savage. This wasn't how he normally was, and he knew it. Lately, his savage nature had taken hold and changed him into someone even he couldn't stand to be around. He was aware that Des had grown to hate being his field partner, hated having to watch him inch his way into a darkness that he'd never return from.

Des climbed onto her bike while Zylan jogged up behind her. He grabbed his wreckage and pushed it beside her. And, as was becoming usual, they limped home in complete silence. As any good field partner would do, Des had tried to talk sense into him, tried to keep him from going over the edge of insanity, but Zylan knew she was wasting her words on him. And from her silence, Zylan knew Des wasn't about to waste any more on him that night. Zylan was broken inside. He was fighting off a future he didn't want and fighting for a woman he did. He was caught between heaven and hell.

It took almost an hour of silence before they landed at the front door of their compound. Des parked her bike and left Zylan standing in the driveway.

Zylan pushed another ruined bike into the garage and washed up in the sink they used when working on equipment or cars. Stepping up to the door, he caught his reflection. His eyes, once dripping in kindness, reminded him of Riam's eyes—complete darkness. He shook it off, put on his party face and stepped inside.

Neri's was the first face he saw, as always. She waited for his return and was the first one to the door. At first he thought she was a breath of fresh air, complete happiness. It took his brain a moment to tell his feet to run in the other direction.

"This stops now," Neri spoke, her voice calm and steady.

Zylan put up his hands and backed up, into Sid. He turned his head. The Watchyr didn't look happy to see him either. He turned back to Neri, who now had Amity at her side, holding her hand.

"You want me to leave the Slayers?" Zylan asked.

She shook her head and lifted her hand to silence him, before he could say anything else. "Don't speak to me as if I'm a fool. You're out there trying to avenge me, yet you show me no respect with simple honesty."

"Neri—" Zylan started. Sid's hand clamped onto his shoulder and stopped his words.

Sid leaned in and whispered, "If you were smart—which you're not—you'd shut your fucking pie hole and listen."

Neri paced in front of Zylan, coming to a stop and closing her eyes. "Zy, you are not a Slayer. You are a killer. I will *not* be with a man who is a killer. You bring *me* no honor like this. You bring *yourself* no honor like this. What you are doing is shameful. You are killing for the sake of killing, but, worse, you're doing this in my name. I won't have it. I don't want it. I do *not* want you like this."

Zylan teetered backward, thankful that Sid was behind him. It felt like he had just been shot in the chest, had his heart ripped out then placed in a blender.

Neri opened her eyes and gave him the soft smile he had grown to know and trust. It told him all could work out.

She shook her head. "I love you, Zy. I love you more than I knew I could, more than I knew love could be. But I love you enough to leave, to walk away and end your need to avenge me. I love myself enough to not want to watch this happen."

Neri turned her back to him. It took her stepping away

from him for him to break. He lunged forward and dropped to his knees, grabbing onto her legs and begging her.

"Please, no. Don't leave me. It can't end like this. Please," Zylan sobbed. "I swear to you, this ends now. I give you my word. I will be the man you want me to be. Please don't leave me."

Neri turned in his grip, lifting his head up to meet her eyes. "I do not want you to be anyone but who you are — the true Zylan-Nefarious Bloodletting. I want you to be a man you can be proud of, someone you'd want your children to be proud of. I want you to be a man of worth and honor."

"Just please don't leave me. *Please,*" Zylan's words barely creaked out. The room slowly started to shift. His sight was burry. "I can't breathe. Oh God, I'm dying."

Zylan released Neri and slid to his side, barely sitting up. He pulled at the collar on his shirt, wheezing and gasping for air.

Neri dropped to her knees beside him. "Zy, you're having a panic attack. Breathe in through your nose, slowly."

He shook his head. "I'm dying, Neri. I can feel it."

Neri pulled his head into her lap, as the room slowly stopped spinning. *Okay, so I'm not about to die.* But the thought of Neri leaving had brought him close enough. Sid helped Neri get Zylan to his bed then he and Amity left them both to sort things out.

He clung to her for the rest of the night. She'd put her foot down, as he'd seen Des do so many times with Cael. And, like Cael, Zylan fell in line and would do whatever was asked of him. He would have chopped off his own limbs if it meant she would stay.

To Zylan, love was nonsensical, but it gave him more than he could have ever hoped to have. Love built hope and gave strength. As much of a weakness as love was, it was the biggest weapon he could ever possess.

Together, with Neri at his side, he felt as if he could conquer the world.

Chapter Fifteen

Leaving the Slayers had been easy.

It'd hurt—an unseen pain unlike anything Amity's heart had ever felt. But it had been easy. She'd stayed long enough to learn how to fhade and to complete the deeds that would sign her death warrant. She'd waited until Sid was on duty, with plans of returning for dinner with her. She'd waved him off and wished him a fine hunt. Standing in her bedroom with her eyes closed, she'd calmed herself. Her pulse had felt like a bunny's, trapped in a snare. Her heart had pounded as if it was trying to escape her flesh, to escape the fate she'd chosen. Taking in a deep breath, she'd gone.

Amity's return to Sola-Nosfer had not been as soothing as she'd once thought it would be. Being sent into Zy's world had frightened her. She'd wanted to go home. That had been all she'd been able to think of. Zylan's world had not been her own. It had been nothing like the life she'd been used to. The smells had made her sick. The sounds had made her skin jump, and reality had been different in the compound. The way they'd all spoken had made her cringe. There had been no order, no respect—nothing that had made her enjoy it there.

That is, until she'd spent time with Sidriel. Soon, the smells had told hidden stories. Then everything was unique within the walls of the compound. The sounds had turned into music. They had been the songs of a freedom Amity had come to learn that she craved. The way each Slayer had spoken had turned into something she'd looked forward to. The Slayers were all equals. They had leadership, not dictatorship. Everyone had a voice and an opinion. No one was shunned for speaking their mind. More than that, they would ask each other to speak up, including herself. Even when she'd spoken out against her mate, she'd not been beaten. She was respected. The world of Zylan was a world of chaos and kindness, deadly but beautiful, like a rose with thorns. Leaving that world had her feeling like she'd left half of herself behind. She'd left the best parts of herself on the floor of her bedroom there.

Amity stood in front of the throne of Sola-Nosfer, trying to calm her raging pulse. She knew this would be over soon. King Rhival-Enmity Bloodletting and Vestal Virgin Queen Zylamon-Vhenom Bloodletting both looked down on her from their grand thrones. The judging eyes of her sovereigns were nothing like the heat coming from her birthing parents. Her father, Vhenom-Ash Blooddawn, a High Councilman, and her mother, Ayla-Dhemise Blooddawn, Vestal Virgyn, stared at her with looks of disgrace and disgust.

Amity knew she'd brought them all shame. Her actions had tarnished her family's name. Her death would be the only way to atone for the dishonor. The part of her that she'd left behind would have fought for her life and her freedom. To the death, she would have clawed her way back. The Slayers had taught her many things. Fighting tooth and nail, even though she might lose, was one of them. But she'd made a promise. She would find a way out of this — for Zylan and Neri. *This is the difference between doing what is right and saving ass, to borrow a term from Sid.*

Amity stood in her usual gauze gown, her bare feet poking out from under the hem. Her toes made her smile, but not enough for anyone to notice. She'd never risk that. But inside, she was smiling ear to ear. Seeing her toenails painted a pale pink with sparkles reminded her of Sid and how he'd given her a pedicure while waiting for her transformation. The memory had solidified her reasons for standing in front of her king and queen, shunned by her people.

The Vestalis Maxima, Phain, with no last name—the overseer of all Vestal Virgyns—stepped forward, her gaze on the floor. "Sire, we have inspected the Vestal Virgyn, Amity. It is true. She is of ruin and corruption. She has broken her vow of chastity and has bedded a male. This male, by her account, was not her mate, the prince."

"Amity-Rhuin Blooddawn," the king finally spoke. His voice, filled with hateful anger, made her ears twitch. "You bring shame to your sacred station, and you have allowed your inner fire to extinguish. The punishment, under law, will be scourging, followed by entombment. May the mighty Orygin have mercy on your soul."

Amity didn't lift her head. No one looked directly at the king or queen. To do so would be considered an insult. She was not their equal. No one was. She didn't have a voice here or an opinion, and no one ever disagreed. She simply nodded. She'd known what her punishment would be. She'd known she'd be lashed until her bones shone under the moonlight. Her bloodied body would be tossed inside the white marble tomb, which would be sealed up after her. A small ration of food and water would be provided. She'd seen this done before. The Vestal Virgyn would survive for about a week. Once dead and gone, the people of Sola-Nosfer would clean the tomb out, open it up and keep it as a warning for the others.

"Do you have any final words?" Queen Zylamon-Vhenom Bloodletting asked.

Amity thought for a moment. *What could I possibly say?*

"Your grace, it was an honor to have served your son, Prince Zylan-Nefarious Bloodletting." She knew she should have stopped there, but that was not what her time with Zy had taught her. *Go to your death with pride, with honor and with a set of balls that will choke your killers.* "He is a fine male, and through him and his warriors, I have found my worth. You may take my light and extinguish the memory of who I am within these walls, but you will never remove what I have given, for him—for his love and for his future."

Before she could continue, the king pounded his hand on the arm of his grand, wooden throne. "Enough!"

With her spine straightened, she lifted her head, looking him dead in the eyes—eyes that once were as kind as she remembered Zylan's to be.

"Sire, I agree—*enough*. I have had enough. I am a being and not your dog to kick. I am no one's dog," Amity said. Her voice was as strong as it had been the very first moment she'd stood tall against Zylan. "Allow me to walk with my head high to my death, for I will not go with my tail tucked between my legs, my King. I will not become another one of your victims. Whether you wish to acknowledge my worth or not, I am more than that."

Everyone in the room sighed in awe. Had they not planned her death already, she would have been struck down and slaughtered on their pretty marble floor. Being a Vestal Virgin, she knew they could kill her in only so many ways. But the king would be tempted. She knew how badly he wanted to take out a knife this very moment and carve out her still-beating heart. She could see it in his eyes.

Amity bowed but caught the queen's eye. The queen hid her surprise and pride from everyone but Amity. Amity knew those governed emotions all too well. Amity knew the queen had wanted to stand up to the king many times, but she couldn't risk leaving her children in the hands of that monster. Amity had watched the queen, always on the verge of opening her mouth and standing up to the man she was forced to call her mate.

Amity followed the Vestalis Maxima, with her head held high, toward her own demise. Amity didn't lower her eyes as she was tied to a post in the middle of the town square for all to watch. With her arms secured above her head, she looked up at the stars and smiled. With each lash that landed on her flesh, she kept her smile. The pain was incredible, but the knowledge of her sacrifice made it less, in some way. The king could command that the lasher strip the meat from her bones, but he'd never remove her sacrifice or her love.

Amity slumped into the post. Held up with the ropes at her wrists, she had remained conscious throughout the first punishment. She'd pushed her hips into the wooden post and had dragged her body to standing. She did as she had watched Riam train the others to do, breathe past the pain. He would tell them, *'Pain is not your enemy. Pain is your friend. Pain lets you know you are still alive. Pain reminds you that you are still in the fight. Pain is only temporary. Death is the only absolute.'*

They removed the ropes binding her wrists. Her arms flopped to her sides, and two men stepped up to drag her to her entombment and ultimate death.

"Unhand me. I will walk under my own steam. I'm not an animal to be packed after a hunt," Amity called out, her voice cracking under the pain. Her chin trembled, and her vision was blurred from tears, but she would be damned before she allowed her lashers to drag her to the tomb.

"Let her go!" the queen yelled from across the courtyard. "If she wishes to walk, she will walk."

Dizzy, Amity shuffled through the crowd, arms held out for balance. She held her head high, painfully, but, nonetheless, it stayed up. She would not dare drop her eyes to the ground. She was a being, with a soul, who would not crawl or beg for mercy. Her mercy would come in the arms of the Orygin. It would come in Elysium. Sid had told her stories of *home*. The thought of the fields of flowers removed just enough of the pain for her to make it to her tomb.

She risked one look back, to the queen. "I forgive you, my Queen."

Queen Zylamon-Vhenom Bloodletting, who was a pillar of schooled emotions—never to recoil or flinch, never to show even the faintest of sentiment—closed her eyes. The moonlight lit the path of tears rolling down her pale cheeks. She placed both hands over her heart and nodded.

Amity stepped into her tomb, a white marble box, small holes drilled up near the top of the walls for air. Candles were lit, sitting on little slabs placed in the marble as shelves. She took a seat on the only bench in the middle and watched as a marble slab door was pushed into place. The farthest wall held food, water, blankets and extra candles.

The scourging held one main purpose, and it wasn't just to inflict angry pain. The pain would create an inability to fhade. When she had no energy and was filled with too much pain, she could not fhade to escape it. But, as a precaution, the room held the smell of herbs, also used to ward off the use of abilities.

Amity looked around her last home and thought, *It could be worse*. Sid had spoken about some of his apartments that would make this place look like a godsend. The last one, in particular, had rats the size of small dogs that would nibble on his toes and fingers while he was passed out in a drunken stupor. She could have done without the claw marks on the marble, but still, it was better than flesh-eating rats. Those would have made her scream and try to claw her way out of here, as the last Vestal Virgyn obviously had clearly tried.

Amity wished she'd spent more time with Sid. He was broken inside. Her leaving would be one more wound he would suffer. But he would have known, in his own way, that she wouldn't be home when he got back. When Sid had been getting ready to go out, he'd kept pausing and staring at her. Before leaving, he'd hugged her, long and hard. His goodbye had been final. It had given her the strength she'd needed to fhade. Even though he'd made plans for her dinner, they were half-hearted, as if he'd known she wouldn't be there to eat it. He'd known she wouldn't be back, and she knew it'd hurt him to know he couldn't interfere with her path. His gift was his biggest curse — to know an outcome and not be able to change it.

Painfully she moved to the back of the tomb, making a bed from the blankets and curling up on the ground. She let the pain take her over and push her into a deep sleep. She could do nothing more than wait for her death. She would face it without fear. She looked forward to Elysium and all of its freedom from pain and anguish.

* * * *

Coming to a dead stop, Zylan could barely breathe. His chest felt tight, like someone was twisting it in their fists. Shaking his head, he put his hand on a tree for balance. Zylan and Sid had been out all night on hunts.

"You solid?" Sid asked, standing in front of Zylan.

Zylan shook his head back and forth. "Something's wrong, Sid, and don't say it's a panic attack. Something is fuckin' wrong. I can feel it in my goddamn bones. Don't you feel it?"

Sid nodded, but gave no clue as to what the hell was going down. "Perhaps we should head back?"

"Neri!" Zylan screamed. The thought that someone was wrong with his Fyrvor had lit a fire under his ass.

They were twenty minutes out, and he was booking it as fast as he could. Sid wasn't chasing behind him. He was walking at his usual Sid speed. Sid didn't chase after fate. Zylan didn't stop to ask questions or slow his own pace. Unlike Sid, Zylan didn't have all the time in the world.

Pushing the front door open, Zylan screamed for Neri. He had to see her, had to make sure she was all right. As Zylan was coming into the hall, Neri was stepping out of the bedroom, her eyes red and puffy.

"What happened? Who did this to you?" Zylan asked, pulling her into his chest.

Part of him was relieved that she was only crying and that it wasn't something worse. But seeing her didn't end the tightness in his chest.

"Amity... She's gone. She left," Neri whispered, still crying. "I was going to get her to watch a movie with me, and I found a letter on her bed."

Zylan jerked back, grabbing the letter from Neri's hand.

To my closest friends,
It is an honor to think of you all as my friends. I've never truly

had a friend, until now. I thank you all for your time and care. I have returned to Sola-Nosfer. I return with a fate that will offer freedom to my Prince and his love, the dearest Neri. I would die one thousand deaths for your love of each other. I thank you for sharing this love with me. It is more than I could have ever prayed for and more than I've ever been gifted.

To my dearest Sidriel, Sid... You have taught me how to be strong, how to be a being. Always remember, you too are a being. Thank you.

Loving you all is what will carry me to my end. Don't be foolish and come for me, as I know you all will wish to. I give myself for your freedom. Please do not allow my sacrifice to be in vain. Allow me this last wish, my dying wish. Allow me true peace and freedom.

Loving you all so dearly,

Amity, no longer a Vestal Virgyn. I am finally free.

Zylan turned to face Sid, who was now leaning against the entrance to the hallway. "You knew, didn't you? You knew she was leaving, and you said nothing!"

Sid didn't respond. There would be no point and nothing that he could possibly say to ease the pain Zylan was feeling.

"The only way she could be entombed is if she gave herself to someone," Zylan snarled, stepping closer to Sid. "What did you do?"

"I did what she asked of me," Sid replied.

Zylan saw red, and he hit Sid with everything he had, square in the jaw. The fallen Watchyr did nothing to protect himself. Zylan rode Sid to the floor, swinging and connecting, over and over, landing blow after blow. And each time Sid did nothing to stop Zylan or to block the blows.

"You killed her!" Zylan screamed into Sid's face. "You couldn't keep your dick in your pants, could you? You couldn't fuckin' wait!" Zylan stood, kicking Sid in the ribs. "You piece of fuckin' shit!"

Neri tried grabbing onto Zylan to pull him back, but

Zylan was like a bull in a china shop. Each time she would grab him, he'd take her with him. She stepped back and shoved off from the wall, tackling Zylan around the waist and bringing him to the floor.

She crawled up his body and grabbed his face. "Enough! We solve *nothing* like this."

Zylan thought about jumping back up but thought again. If he moved, he'd hurt his Neri. He'd sooner lay on the floor and let Sid kick his ass than harm a hair on her beautiful head.

"You and I both know Sid can't intervene. He can't change fate any more than we can. Stop this. Stop this right fuckin' now," Neri yelled into his face. "If you want some truth, Sid was the only one here who truly loved her. He gave her what she needed, knowing you'd hate him, knowing he'd lose her. You honor that sacrifice. You do *not* punish it."

Sid rolled off of the floor, using his shirt to clean the blood from his face. He moved to Zylan's side, extending his hand as he gazed out of the hallway into the meeting room. "Zy, your mother is here."

Chapter Sixteen

It had been ten years since Zylan had seen his mother. To him, ten years was still too soon. He'd thought the next time he would lay eyes upon her would be as they strapped him to the table before she dragged a blade across his throat. *Apparently now is a better time.* As usual, her timing was perfection. Choosing the moment when his heart was hurting, because of that godforsaken curse — the curse she'd placed on him the day he'd been birthed.

Queen Zylamon-Vhenom Bloodletting stood in the main hall, hands clasped in front of her hips. Her posture was perfect — the still statue she was trained to be. Her hair was tied up in a perfect series of knots, not a hair out of place. Her gown, blood red and to her toes, was set perfectly on her flawless frame. Nothing about her was out of place, aside from where she was currently standing.

"My son." She spoke two words that made his skin crawl.

"Mother," Zylan spat out. The word came with more hate now than ever before.

"I see you have heard the news of your Amity?"

"She was not mine. She belonged to no one." Zylan glared. "What the hell do you want?"

If Zylan hadn't known what he was looking for, he'd have missed the millisecond of emotion that flashed behind her eyes. But he saw it. He wanted it to bother her. He wanted her to feel something and show it, for once.

"Perhaps if your father had shown me the same care and attention that you all have shown Amity, things would have been different for us all. But that was not the case. What do I want? I have come to request that you complete your

Reaping, to save Amity. I have come to request your death. It is only with that death that you will have true power and can create the change you wish to see."

Zylan's mouth dropped open. He hadn't been expecting this. He expected his death, yes, but to save Amity? He wasn't expecting that in the least. He didn't think his mother gave a flying fuck.

"She stood tall, something I was unable to do. She is brave, something I am unable to be. She walked to her death with honor," his mother's voice hinted at a crack of emotion. Her eyes blinking rapidly, trying to draw back in the tears that now glittered in her eyes. "With your death, you may order her release. I have come to ask this of you. You owe me nothing, but you owe her, my son. She should not die like this—not alone in the dark, in pain and starvation."

Neri jabbed Zylan in the ribs. "Either you go, or I will go with a loaded gun. I don't care how, but she comes home. But keep in mind that if I go, I'll likely burn the place to the ground and kill us all, but I'll die knowing that I went to bring our girl home."

"I'd have to give you up. I don't think I can do that," Zylan whispered, feeling his throat tighten.

Neri touched his cheek, her soft smile filling him with calm. "She has sacrificed her life for our love, Zy. We will find a way."

"I will await your decision. You have but days, my son." His mother stepped away, her shoulders hunched. Her pride had been beaten out of her centuries ago.

"Mother," Zylan called out to her. As she turned, he added, "Thank you."

Pain was painted on her face for all to see. In that moment, she hid nothing. "I have failed you, my son. I will not fail her. If you cannot return, please inform me at once, and I will release her myself."

"Father will kill you for it," Zylan reminded her.

She nodded and smiled. "It would be an honorable death—one I would welcome after all of these years."

Zylan watched his mother walk out, the front door closing behind her. He gripped Neri's hand and walked away silently, knowing it was all finally coming to an end. Their love, however strong it was, would be tested in the worst of ways, by separation and death.

* * * *

Sid stepped into Amity's bedroom, letting her smell fill his lungs. Kneeling beside her bed, he touched her sheets. He could also feel the heat she'd left behind. The temptation to intervene was stronger than his will to live. If there had been a chance he could save his friends without risking their souls, he would have done it in a heartbeat. He forced his eyes to close and willed his mind home, when what he'd wanted to do could have damned them all to Hades.

He opened his eyes in Elysium. At one time, he'd thought of home as the most beautiful thing he'd ever seen, but this was no longer true. Amity was — and always would be — the most beautiful thing he would ever lay his eyes on. Home had lost its glow when he compared it to the way Amity's hair shone in the candlelight. Even her eyes made the colors here seem paler and more basic.

"I know what you have come to ask, Sidriel," the Orygin spoke, this time as a young man. The Orygin was never the same person twice, with varying sex and age. Sid never knew if the Orygin was a man or a woman and had never thought to ask.

Sid knelt on the ground, the flowers brushing his arms, reminding him of how Amity's touch had tickled his skin. "I beg of you. Allow me to help my friends. Allow me to save Amity and keep Zylan from his Reaping."

"It is not out of righteous duty that you wish to help. If it were, you would not be here asking this of me. You would simply do it. It is out of love, which I am grateful you have finally found. But as you know, a Watchyr may love all of humanity but can never walk the same path as a mortal."

Before Sid could argue that Amity and Zylan were Vampyre and not truly mortal, the Orygin spoke again. "If you can end their existence, they are mortal. You are a Watchyr, Sidriel. Their world is not your world. Your very love for them, as individuals, is a risk. You are blinded by love. That blindness tempts your hand, tempts you to meddle with their destiny. I can feel your desire to change paths already written."

There was no winning. Either he didn't love them enough or he loved them too much. *Where the fuck is the balance?* Sid dropped his head, wanting to scream and beat his fists into the flowers, ruining them.

"Scream, curse, burn the fields, flood our valley. It will not change their fate, Sidriel."

Sid pounded his fists into the ground and spun, facing the Orygin. He lifted his face, wet with tears. "I beg of you, please. I will give you anything you ask of me, anything. I don't want Zylan to give his first life and his one true love, to save Amity. He doesn't want that life and Amity doesn't want that sacrifice. I need to help them."

"My dear Sidriel, Zylan has already agreed to complete his Reaping, to save Amity. Nerissa knows she may never have her love. Their destiny is set. We do not alter their paths, you know this. I feel your pain. Your need to help them is suffocating. You have danced too close to intervening too many times. If you continue these ways, those you care for will die. I can see it."

He sobbed, hanging his head. He wanted to save the day. For once, he wanted to do something and not just stand there. Instead, Zylan would die his first death, Neri would be without her mate, and Amity would forever hate that she was saved at such an expense.

The Orygin, now a young woman mirroring Amity, touched his shoulder. "I can feel how your heart beats for Amity. You have gotten too close, Sidriel. You will say goodbye, before your actions are her ending. Out of my own love for my child, I will remove her memory of that love. She will never remember your love—only you will remember. She will be your reminder of how closely you have come to altering fate."

Sid nodded. He knew Amity had known of his temptation to intervene to save her, Zylan and Neri. He'd contemplated it before going home. And now he would need to give her up. He would walk away from the Fyrvor he could never have as a reminder of how close he had come to risking them all. He didn't bother arguing. He knew the Orygin was right.

Sid opened his eyes in Amity's bedroom, on his knees, still gripping the sheets. Then in one blink, he had his arms wrapped around Amity, on the floor of the tomb. Sid breathed in her scent. He would remember this smell for all times. This had to be the darkness he had felt coming—the bone-crushing pain of losing someone, willingly—for he couldn't envision anything worse happening to him.

"I believe the fat lady is singing," Amity whispered, pulling his arms tighter around her. He noticed her wince once at the pressure now on her back, as she drifted back to sleep.

Sid breathed in her scent. He would remember this smell for all of his days. He knew, as time went on, he would catch a hint of it, and it would bring him back to this moment.

He held her, hoping that somehow him being here would be enough. He knew it wouldn't, but he couldn't help but hope, because that was what love did. It pushed him to hope. Sid would take whatever love dished out, including a suffering that he'd carry for the rest of all days.

"I love you," Sid whispered into Amity's ear.

"You will say goodbye to her, Sidriel," the Orygin whispered through the tomb.

Looking around, he saw more food and supplies were sitting in a large basket. At the end of the tomb, by the door, the Orygin stood.

Sid lifted his head. "I thought you wouldn't save her?"

The Orygin nodded. "I'm not the one saving her or anyone

else. Zylan is giving his first life for her, and through that, Neri may give up her first love, for Amity. My gift to you is time to say goodbye. Now what is your sacrifice? Will you still give your love for her? What will you give to ensure balance? My gifts do not come without a price for us all."

Sid nodded. "I will give my love."

The Orygin smiled. "You will always have that love, as a reminder of true sacrifice. But you will never be permitted to build on it. She will not remember, will not love you in return. That is the sacrifice. You must say goodbye."

Sid nodded again. "I will do it."

"And so shall it be done. You will have until the tomb is opened once again to spend time with her. She will remember you, but she will not remember your heart or hers. It is the deepest sacrifice. You will be the only one with the knowledge of the love you once shared. No one else will remember this. If ever she learns of this love, she will perish. Is this still your wish?"

Sid closed his eyes and let out a shaking breath. "Yes, it's worth it. Plus, everyone grows to hate me anyway. This should be relatively easy."

"I would certainly hope so, in this case."

The Orygin was gone as suddenly as she had appeared. Sid clung to Amity. They could love until that door opened again. Selfishly, he didn't want it to open again. But when it did, he was ready to let her go. He wondered how long it would take before they would come to clean it out? A week, perhaps? If he was lucky, they'd have two weeks. He knew that the Slayers would be here and busting the place open within days, if not hours.

Sid climbed out from behind Amity and grabbed the supplies left by the Orygin. Rolling her onto her stomach, he slathered ointment from the basket onto her. By the time she woke, she would be healed. He placed food out for her, in case she woke and was hungry. Climbing back into place, wrapping himself around her, he slept with his face pressed into her hair, breathing in the smell of his Amity, the Fyrvor he would never have.

Chapter Seventeen

Lying nude, on his back on a marble slab at Sola-Nosfer, Zylan shook like a ragdoll. His hand was locked in a death grip around Neri's. When it came time for him to return for the Reaping, Neri had refused to stay behind at the compound. The queen had allowed Neri to come — something she would be punished for later — allowing an outsider and making a decision without consulting the king. But in true fashion, his father would not allow the others to think it wasn't his own decision. He'd sooner put on a front and beat his wife later than appear weak in any way. His mother knew what was coming, but she'd stood firm, not backing down.

The Slayers would not be permitted to attend. They were not his people. One person his father would tolerate, but not more. Zylan had tried to find Sid, to ask him to attend, but Sid was nowhere to be found. Sid could blend. He could hide. Zylan's father couldn't kick out someone he couldn't find.

There were plenty of tears shed when Zylan left. Neri would be back to the compound once the ceremony was completed and he was locked away with five donors who would help him when he awoke, bloodthirsty. Once his Reaping was complete, Zylan would find a way to come and go, to be with her. They'd have to drag him into the sun to keep him from her. Bottom line, he'd do this to save Amity and for no other reason. He knew he owed her this — and more. He hoped he wasn't too late.

Neri knelt beside Zylan, her soft smile keeping him planted. Without her, they would have needed to drug him and tie him down. On his other side, his brother knelt with his wife, a Vestal Virgyn. His brother was one of the lucky few who had fallen head over heels for his chosen mate. And she, in turn, loved him back. Tonight, her usual smiling face was marred in grief for Amity. All the Vestal Virgyns were in mourning.

He couldn't shake the tightness in his chest. It had been there for days. Like a dark shadow weighing down his shoulders. He was about to die. It didn't get any darker than that. Lights out in less than ten minutes… He just wanted to get it over and done with. Instead, his father droned on and on about the new age coming. When Zylan woke, he would be crowned king. That part, he was looking forward to. He would release Amity. He would restore her honor then he would release her and the other Vestal Virgins, abolishing the tradition, once and for all. Those who wished to stay could stay, but there would be some fucking changes around Sola-Nosfer. Any act of abuse toward any man, woman or child would be treated as an act of aggression toward the crown, toward the king.

Neri rubbed her thumb over his shaking hand. "I'm right here. I love you."

Zylan's brother Zander held his other hand, squeezing it tightly. "I'm sorry, brother. If I could take your place, I would."

Zylan smiled. "I know you would."

Zander leaned into Zylan's ear, whispering, "Zylan, don't give up hope. I think I've found a loophole. I've been reading old text. I'll keep digging. I give you my word. I won't stop until I've exhausted all leads."

Zander had been trying to find a way for Zylan to get out of having to give up Neri to take the throne.

Zylan squeezed his brother's hand. "It's too late, but do me one small kindness. Keep hold of your Fyrvor and never let her go. Treat her well. Treat her with honor and dignity. Treat her as we would have wished our mother to have been treated."

"I always have and always will, or may I be struck down by the Orygin," Zander answered, staring at his father. Zander, like Zylan, hated his father for what he did to their mother. Zander lifted his hand, motioning toward the room. "It's time."

"Fuck," Zylan groaned.

His mind went back to every Reaping he'd witnessed before he'd left. He remembered how proud the family members were. He recalled toasting to their death, celebrating, as though they hadn't just killed someone. To his people, this wasn't a killing. This was a rebirthing. They saw it as shedding the skin of the first life then proudly being carried into the new life. This didn't feel anything like that. This felt like his death, like he was giving away something precious. It was one of the ten million reasons he'd chosen to leave.

Even though he was doing this to save Amity—who'd given everything for him—he was still scared. His stomach flopped, and his lungs constricted. He was on the verge of puking and passing out. *Maybe I'll pass out as I'm puking. Won't that make for a great first death?* His father would probably die of embarrassment. It was a win-win.

Neri pushed her face into Zylan's sightline then winked. "You've got this. Just one more mission. Only this time, I'm right beside you. Of course, I'll go eventually, before you start to stink. It's almost impossible to get that smell from my hair."

Zylan grinned, letting out a small laugh. "Vampyres do not break down. There is no rigor mortis, smart-ass."

"Oh? And when did you go to Vampyre medical school?"

He pulled her mouth to his, kissing her with the last bit of his life. "I love you, Neri, with my entire being. No matter what, I'll always find my way back home, back to you."

She placed her hand over his heart. "I'll be waiting. Don't be late."

Zylan's mother stepped to the head of the slab and lowered to her knees. Her hand shook as she held onto the golden blade. Looking up at her eyes, Zylan could see the tears falling. It wasn't like her to show this kind of emotion in front of everyone. She would be punished for this and likely punished again for deserving a second punishment in the same day. There was no pleasing his father, no pleasing any of the men of Sola-Nosfer.

Lifting his hand to hers, he squeezed. "I love you."

Relief, for once. She looked relieved, like a weight had been lifted from her shoulders.

"Thank you for Neri. I'm sorry for what you'll endure because of it," Zylan whispered.

She smiled. He couldn't remember the last time he'd seen his mother smile. "I can take it," she said. "Once you take the throne, I'm very sure I'll never have to take it again."

"You can bet the fuckin' farm on it. Never a-fuckin-gain." Zander spoke up, angry that his mother would be treated like a hated animal later. He looked to his mother. She hated when he cursed. "I apologize for the language, Mother."

Neri kissed Zylan one more time then leaned back. She looked to his mother and gave her a soft smile and a nod. They were all ready.

His mother spoke in old tongue, a language he remembered from his childhood. His mother used to tell him stories while sitting with him in a blanket fort. He opened his mind to the memories he treasured most — trips hunting with his brother, his first few weeks with Cael and Riam and the moment he'd first laid eyes on Neri. He thought of Sid and the pain he carried and of Bane, howling at the moon when he thought no one was looking. He recalled arm-wrestling with Ester, the queen of poor bedside manner, and of every time his ass was pulled out of hot water by Riam. He let those memories flood his mind as he said goodbye to his first life.

When the blade did its deed, it was hot at first. Then it stung. Zylan tried not to fight it, not to thrash, but his body had its own ideas. He couldn't breathe. Each wheezing breath was filled with hot blood. His eyes widened and finally focused on Neri. There was no fear on her face. Her smile stopped his body from its violent shakes. She didn't cry or shirk away. She was his stone to hold on to.

"I'm right here, Zy. I've got you," Neri yelled over the sound of clapping spectators and the upper crust of his society. "I love you!"

Zylan mouthed the words back. His mouth parted, as his body struggled for the air it would never get. His body contracted and released, fighting for the life it would never find. With each blink, the world grew darker. He felt his body grow cold and numb, but he could still feel Neri's hand in his.

"Don't be late, Zy. You promised," Neri whispered into his ear. "I love you. We *will* meet again."

Zy closed his eyes. His last vision was of the woman he loved. With that image, he'd find the strength to come back to her. He would fight to return. He wouldn't be late. He was gone with the last of his blood dripping down the slab, filling a golden bowl. The bowl was collected and would be used to fill the glasses for the first toast of the night.

* * * *

Neri stared, her eyes now coated in tears and her mouth agape. She'd forced herself not to cry when Zylan would have been aware of it. She would be strong for him. She knew he would need it. Hands touched her shoulders, to pull her back from Zylan. She shook her head. She wasn't ready yet.

Zander came around to her side, batting away the hands that touched Neri's shoulders. "He must be prepared, Neri, or he will not return. His transformation must begin now, or all is lost."

Neri nodded, lifting Zylan's hand to her lips, kissing his palms. "Don't be late."

Neri stumbled backward and watched as six men lifted

Zylan off the slab then carried him over their shoulders toward the back of the hall, while the partygoers sang songs in a language she didn't understand. Behind Zylan, five women, who could die but had volunteered to be his first feast, followed. They, like him, were Vampyre and could sustain a brutal attack by a newborn Vampyre.

As though his mother could read Neri's thoughts, she stepped forward and touched Neri's arm. "There will be no mating. Their blood will bring him back to the Zylan you know and love. After the initial feedings, he will be able to go to your throat, as only a mate should."

Neri nodded. "Thank you for this. Thank you."

"You must return home now, for this is not a place for a human. The events will grow, and they will not be to your taste." She turned to Zander. "Zander, can you please ensure Nerissa is seen safely into her territory?"

Neri staggered as she was being led from the banquet hall. She'd just watched the love of her life killed in front of her, and she'd held his hand as he'd died. Now she would have to wait to see if he was strong enough to return. As bizarre as that experience had been, she was numb.

* * * *

Neri didn't remember the drive home. It happened in a blink. She stepped out of the truck and watched Zander drive away. Zander had spoken to her, but she didn't remember what he'd said. Her mind was miles away – with Zylan. She turned to find Riam lifting her into his arms. Another blink and she was being tucked into the bed she'd shared with Zylan. Another blink and Ester, the resident doc, was sitting on the bed, checking her pulse.

"You're in shock, Neri," Ester spoke. "I'm going to put you out for a bit. Your pulse is bouncing all over the place. You need rest. You need to sleep and not to stare at the ceiling for twenty-eight hours straight."

Over a day had passed, but it had felt like she'd just been

laid down. She had enough smarts to know that Ester was right. She nodded her head and pulled her arm out of the blankets. She looked down at her hand, still caked in Zylan's blood. She squeezed her eyes closed, letting the tears roll. Ester stuck her with a needle and rubbed her arm.

"Don't be late, Zy," Neri whispered as the drugs took over.

Her eyes were too heavy to hold open. Her body felt like a few bags of cement had been placed on top of her limbs. Slowly, she drifted off, mumbling.

Chapter Eighteen

It was a nice night for a stroll through the forest, Strain thought to himself, as his feet pushed through the two-foot-high straw. With each step he could hear the earth crush and the grass rub together. Little pinecones were now buried in the ground to grow into the trees they were meant to become, only for the human pillagers to chop them down to make more fuckin' toothpicks.

Humanity had plundered this earth into miles and miles of bare, bruised land. Holes sat where mountains had once stood. Acid rain now filled the ponds where animals drank. Dams were built, and land was starved of water. *Cha-ching* was the only sound that mattered out in the real world. If it didn't come with a wad of cash, it didn't fuckin' matter. At least Strain could respect the brutal honesty of the real world, if only they'd stop prettying it up as something it wasn't.

Running his fingertips over the long, dry grass, he knew the night held so many possibilities. A small drizzle brought out the smells of the earth, reminding Strain of morning hunts and camping trips. The foul stench from his puppets kept him from venturing too far into his childhood sweetness.

He'd spent the week planning an attack on Sola-Nosfer, the true home of one of the Slayers. Tonight he was putting all of his eggs in one basket. He'd heard that Zylan had returned to Sola-Nosfer and was completing the Reaping. Zylan's first death would leave his fellow Slayers in mourning. They would remain in mourning until they heard if he'd made it through his transformation. Slayers in mourning meant an unguarded city. Now was the time to strike. There would be no better time to wound the Slayers than by taking out one of their strongest — Zylan — while he couldn't defend himself.

The Slayers would be scattered each morning in their own traditions. Their rotations were down to the bare minimum, and each fight had lasted longer than it should have. They weren't in the game, not completely. Strain hadn't seen them roaming the streets lately. They were down to a skeleton crew.

Strain knew that sadness did that to a person, pulled their mind in too many directions for them to give it their all. *It kicked them in the balls and left them hanging in pain.* Strain would bank on this flaw, just as he would expect them to count on his. Any good general would have attacked in this moment. To win the war, he'd use any advantage he could find. He'd have boiled bunnies and taken candy from a baby if it would have helped in the slightest of ways. Strain had read enough books to know how wars were won. And fairness was not a chapter in that book.

Sun Tzu said, *"The opportunity to secure ourselves against defeat lies in our own hands, but the opportunity of defeating the enemy is provided by the enemy himself."*

Strain knew Cael, knew how weak his heart was. Cael wouldn't risk another member while still reeling from the loss of one of his closest. Cael was handing Strain this victory on a silver platter. He'd take it, then send the platter back with the heads of Cael's loved ones.

The Rancor Order was out in full force. Every Proletaryan he'd created was with them. They shuffled through the trees behind Strain. This would be a massacre that would go down in the books. It would be a fight unlike any they'd seen, and it would serve as a final warning not to fuck with Strain or the Order.

Leading his team through the trees, he came to his final stop. Strain would not enter the fight. He wasn't stupid. Strain would have been zeroed in on and targeted. Sola-

Nosfer would leave the rest of the Order alone and hunt Strain down. *Why fight on the front lines when I have expendables to do it for me?*

Strain was placing Garm in charge. Garm was itching to take command of a fight as large as this one. He wanted to prove his worth, which he had, time and time again. But Garm wanted more. He hungered for more. Even though he'd been a dependable Calyph, Garm was unbalanced, like most of his men. But lately Strain had noticed that Garm had an edge on him that sent off warning flares in Strain's mind. Garm loved this just a little too much. He looked forward to this a little more than he should.

Sure, Strain liked a good fight and relished the demise of irregulars, but rolling in dead bodies was going a little too far. Having a wall of skeletal remains was also a little more than insane. He'd recently seen that Garm's apartment was filled with bones and hair and old belongings of those he'd killed and tortured. Bluntly, Garm was getting fucked up. Each day brought Strain closer to questioning the man's sanity. But until the time came where Garm finally lost his grip on reality, he was a tool that Strain needed and knew how to use. Maybe the guy just needed a fuckin' vacation, with medication and a therapist. He made a mental note to rethink making Garm a partner in The Hemlock.

"Welcome to Sola-Nosfer. Let the games begin," Strain called out, pointing to the trees ahead of them. He took no additional steps forward. He turned to his puppets and ordered, "Kill them all."

Wave after wave of his creations flew past Strain as he walked away, whistling into the night. Little raindrops kissed his cheeks, reminding him of rainstorms as a child. He reminisced as he made his way back to the road, into his car and back to Blood Alley. He was in an unusually chipper mood tonight. He ordered his usual drink, sat in his usual chair and enjoyed the view in his soon-to-be club. Tonight was a good night, a great night actually. He motioned toward the first piece of regret on stilettos that he encountered and pointed down to his cock. Normally he'd have waltzed her into the backroom, but tonight he was feeling especially cocky.

Her greed for money and drugs sent her running at him, almost toppling over on her five-inch spiked heels. She was on her knees and had him down her starved throat before his drink hit the table. She held onto the chair as he throat-fucked her. Her arms, covered in track marks, made him hate her just a little more. She would add him to her list of regrets, if she lived that long. They never did, though. They were long dead before they realized just how much he hated them.

Sinking in for the long haul, he sighed. Sola-Nosfer, an empire thousands of years old, would be wiped from the face of this earth in under an hour. Along with Zylan, Slayer Prince, the one who'd taken Neri from him. *What goes around comes around.*

"Take from me. I take from you. You can't hide from fate," Strain whispered to himself, holding onto the head between his legs and pushing it down until she gagged. It was music to his bastard ears.

Chapter Nineteen

Amity woke up to the faintest sounds of screaming. Sid was out cold behind her. He had come to be with her while she died, yet she felt stronger than ever. Her wounds were completely healed. She had complete focus and knew she could fhade, if she wanted to. Her ears twitched to the sound of more screaming. There were no celebrations happening, but something else bad was going on. The darkness was here. The darkness had come. She could feel it in her bones.

Amity closed her eyes and focused her mind. Feeling Sid trying to hold on to her, she pushed herself to fhade. She heard Sid whisper goodbye as she left him.

Amity landed close to the walls of Sola-Nosfer, and she quickly took cover. The walls were crawling with Proletaryans and the Order. Her people were being slaughtered. The buildings flowed with Vampyre warriors, but against the Proletaryans, they stood no chance. She calmed her mind, and pushed herself toward Neri — not her body, just her mind. Neri, in a deep sleep, heard her call and heard her message.

* * * *

Neri opened her eyes to the feeling of someone sitting beside her. A small lamp in the corner offered just enough light to see who it was.

"Amity?" Neri whispered, trying to sit up but feeling like someone was sitting on her chest.

Amity sat beside Neri, her hair in soft curls down her back. She was wearing a white gauze gown. The back of her gown was covered in dry blood and torn cotton, hanging in strips.

"What's happened to you?" Neri whispered then realized that if Amity was out, it meant that Zylan was the king, and he'd ordered her release.

Amity shook her head, as though she could hear Neri's thoughts. She leaned in and whispered to Neri, "Zylan still sleeps. He is on the verge of waking, but it will be too late."

"Too late? For you?"

Amity shook her head again. "You are the only one I can contact, for you hold a piece of my soul. You need to wake up, Neri. You need to wake up and take a message to the others for me. A war is coming. They will kill Zylan and his people. Please, Neri, you need to wake up."

Neri frowned. She was still sleeping.

Amity lunged toward her, pushing a vision into Neri's mind. "Wake up, Neri!"

Neri jerked when Amity's body slammed into hers, bringing her out of a dead sleep, screaming. Riam was the first to get to her, grabbing her arms and trying to hold her down.

"I have a message from Amity," Neri said, struggling under Riam's hands.

Ester stepped back into the room, preparing another needle. "Hush now. It's gonna be okay. We'll fix you right up."

Neri locked eyes with Riam. "Riam, I've had a vision. Amity came to me with a message. She says Sola-Nosfer is under attack. The Rancor Order and the Proletaryans have breached their walls."

Cael skidded into the bedroom and blocked Ester's path.

"Bane. Where's Bane?" Neri yelled. Riam finally let go of her.

"I'm back here, Neri," Bane called back from the group of Slayers who'd come running the moment they'd heard her scream.

"Amity needs you to go to your people. She said she will

be using a charm." Neri was confused, but gave him the message verbatim.

"Done," Bane said and hightailed it out of there, leaving behind the smell of heat and wolf.

Neri sat herself up, pulling her legs out of the blankets, and used Riam to help her stand. She was still dizzy from the drug-induced sleep session.

"Where do you think you're going?" Cael asked her, stepping in her way.

"You will either move willingly or by force," Neri spoke, her voice commanding. "That's my Fyrvor up there. You'll be hurting something fuckin' fierce if you don't move, now."

Cael grinned at her backbone, until Des touched his shoulder.

"Move, Cael, or I will help her," Des spoke, squeezing his shoulder. "How would you like to think you were on fire, Cael?"

Cael stepped aside, grabbing Des and kissing her harshly. "Ballbuster."

Neri looked to Riam. "Can you please help me put on gear?"

Riam nodded and helped her out of the room. The others were moving and moving fast. Cael would fhade in and out, bringing intel back with him. It was dangerous for him to fhade into an unknown location that was under siege. Remaining could be a death sentence. The Slayers would not risk Cael or dropping their numbers.

"Has anyone seen Sid?" Cael yelled out, running for the front door.

Neri smiled. "He's been with Amity since she was entombed, so she wouldn't be alone."

Soon they were geared up and ready to rock, but it would take almost an hour to get there.

* * * *

"Burn them!" Amity screamed, running toward the guards, pointing at the revenant zombies climbing the walls—the Proletaryans. "You must burn them!"

She was ignored, as the honorless whore they'd called her. They pushed her aside. She watched the Sola-Nosfer soldiers march to their deaths. They would not leave Zylan behind. Zylan couldn't be disturbed during his transformation, or he would die. But, in turn, the soldiers would die. Because they wouldn't listen to her, they would all die. She could feel it. She watched the walls crawl with darkness. She watched it flood down into the streets, leaving broken pieces of bodies and pools of blood in their wake.

Focusing, Amity pushed herself to fhade into the woods, away from the danger, into Therian territory. She ran toward the wolves. Holding up her charm bracelet, she ran, screaming for Bane.

"Amity!" Bane called back from deep in the woods.

"Help us! Help!" Amity screamed, running toward his voice.

Hitting a small clearing, she ran straight into Bane, holding her charm, shaking. "I seek your help, the help of your people. I give you my charm, please. Help us, please."

With a sharp whistle, Bane pulled the charm from the bracelet and tossed it behind him. He handed Amity a gun and three extra clips. He didn't bother asking if she knew how to use it. She was trained in everything else. "Move it. We're coming, Amity."

"Thank you, dear Orygin. Thank you," Amity whispered. She turned and ran back to Sola-Nosfer, back toward the darkness.

Inches from the walls of Sola-Nosfer, Amity stopped and calmed herself. She fhaded, feeling the wolves rushing past her, their heat licking up her legs. On the other side of the wall, she opened the gates, letting the wolves flood the streets of the place she'd once called home.

She didn't stop there. As tired as she was, she kept running, running toward the banquet hall, where she knew

Zylan would be housed. It was a bloodbath inside. The Rancor Order was slaughtering women and children who had taken shelter within the safety of the hall.

Amity pulled the trigger three times, before pushing herself into another fhade. She would rematerialize, only to pull the trigger again and fhade. She cleared the room but not soon enough. Everyone was dead. She turned in a circle. Bodies covered the once-white marble floor.

"Amity?" a voice called from the back.

Amity turned with her gun up, as the thick velvet curtains parted. Neri stepped out, holding a gun. Behind her, the queen followed with a small group of children behind her. A small gun was clutched in her shaking and blood-soaked hand.

"Neri." Amity smiled. "How did you get here so fast?"

Neri smiled. "I have my ways, which included grabbing Sid once he'd showed up and pulling him into my bedroom. I may have held a gun to his…important male bits."

Amity grinned and gave Neri a nod, then looked to the queen. "Where is Zander? I know he came back. Where is he hiding?"

The queen shook her head. "I don't know. It all happened so fast. I grabbed as many children as I could carry and ran. Dearest Orygin, I don't even know where my own child is."

"I haven't seen him. I found the queen under attack. Her mate left her to die. I got her in here, tucked her away and have been collecting children and stashing them," Neri said, pointing behind her. "We have twenty more little ones back here. The Order followed me in and killed the others."

Amity nodded and whistled a high-pitched whistle. A Therian skidded into the room, sliding on the blood. The werewolf was Bane. His colors were exactly like his human hair, soft, light browns and shiny. But it was his eyes that told Amity. His eyes were still Bane.

"It's okay. He's with me," Amity said, looking back at Queen Zylamon, who had stepped back in fear. Therians and Vampyres didn't have the best of history. Amity looked back to Bane. "Protect them with your life, Bane, no matter what. I'm going to go find Zander."

"It's all right, Zylamon. Bane is one of the good guys," Neri whispered, pulling them all back behind the thick curtains.

Bane sniffed the air and gave Amity a growl, reminding her to use her senses, to remember how to track. Amity winked and breathed in the air. She breathed past the blood and fear and anger. She breathed in deeply enough to smell Zylan. She could smell the oils they had used on his skin before the Reaping, royal oils. Then she caught the essence of Zander and his wife.

Amity breathed out and fhaded, landing inches from Zander's face.

"Amity!" Zander grabbed her and pulled her behind him, holding his sword out in front of him. Behind him, his wife was holding two scared and crying children.

Amity stepped back to his side. "Zander, we need to go. We can't stay in here. I have brought the Therians, and the Slayers are not far behind. If we have a chance, we need to get the hell out of here. Can you fhade?"

"We can, but the kids… The kids can't fhade yet," Zander replied.

Amity whistled two high-pitched whistles once again, calling two Therians to her location. She grabbed the two kids and moved toward the wolves.

"What are you doing?" Zander snapped, trying to take back his children.

"They have come to help us, Zander. They will get your kids to their territory. You will grab your mother and do the same thing," Amity said, placing the two children onto the backs of the wolves. She looked each wolf in the eyes. "Fight with your lives. You keep them alive, dear Orygin. You keep them alive. Now go!"

Zander's wife screamed, chasing after them. Zander grabbed her hand, pulling her back into his chest, trying to calm her down, reassuring her that the children were safer with the Therians than in Sola-Nosfer. They both pushed themselves into a fhade, Amity followed next.

Rematerializing back in the hall, Amity saw that Neri was standing beside the body of the king, her gun still smoking from pulling the trigger. She looked up to Amity and Zander. "No one gets to abuse me or those I love. I don't care what your station is. No one fuckin' touches me or Zylamon."

Behind her, on the floor, the queen held her gown to her now-bleeding nose.

"She wouldn't leave the children, me or Zylan. She wouldn't leave, so he hit her. He hit her again, and I warned him. He hit her again, so I pointed my gun at him. He grabbed my arm, and I pulled the trigger," Neri explained.

Zander touched Neri's arm and nodded. "Like a dog, he had to be put down." He looked to Bane and winked. "No offense."

Bane howled, his people slinking in behind him. Amity and the others helped load the children onto the backs of the Therians. They were being carried out and into Therian territory. The survivors would fhade and meet them there.

"We have to go," Amity said, grabbing Neri's hand.

Neri shook her head, standing in front of the door to Zylan's transformation chamber. "I won't leave him, Amity. Go, please. Find the others. Save your people. I will save him."

Amity gave Neri a hug and ran from the room. There would be no argument with Neri's plan that could be won. Amity didn't bother wasting the time.

* * * *

Neri stood in front of the door. Each member of the Order who'd made the mistake of venturing too far into the back of the banquet hall had ended up in a pool of his own brains. With her Fyrvor behind that door, she could do this all night and all day without needing a break.

Bane returned, taking a seat to her right. Neri grabbed hold of his fur and waited. Anyone who entered was taken out, fast and hard. They spared no one, gave no warnings and took no chances.

Bane tilted his head, growling. Neri's mouth twisted into a grin. "They're going to be so fucking sorry."

Neri and Bane stepped to the side as they heard Zylan let out a blood-curdling scream. She'd never heard a more frightening sound, but she welcomed it. The door came off of its hinges, sliding across the floor, stopping against the bodies.

Zylan emerged and took one look at Neri, who gave him a nod, and he was gone. Neri jumped onto Bane's back, and they both were off, running behind Zylan. Sola-Nosfer was ablaze. The Slayers were here in full force, bring the Proletaryans to their deaths, but the damage was already done. There weren't many survivors. The grounds were twisted heaps of Vampyres and bad guys. Neri climbed off Bane once the coast was clear. She walked beside the wolf, trying to be careful not to step on all the remains.

Zylan, with someone dragging behind him, came back to Neri. He kissed her lips. "I told you I wouldn't be late." He tossed a man to Neri's feet. "Is this the man who helped torture you?"

Neri stepped back. "Zylan, don't do this. You swore to me."

"Neri, answer the question, please."

Even though she knew his 'please' was added for effect, Neri closed her eyes, nodding her head, over and over. She was back in Strain's prison. She was back in the room. "His name is Garm. He is a Calyph. Please, Zy. Don't do this. Not for me and not in my name."

Zylan grabbed Neri and pulled her into his arms. "I gave my word."

Neri opened her eyes. Garm was being bound by Riam and guarded by Bane. By the sight of Bane's raised hackles, he wanted Garm to bolt. He wanted to chase him down and rip him limb from limb.

"Let's go, Neri. Neither of us needs to see this," Zylan whispered, turning her around and walking her away.

She didn't flinch when she heard Garm scream. She truly didn't care. She just didn't want it to stain her or her Fyrvor.

"All of my family, they're gone. I used to wish for them to just be gone, but not like this—never like this," Zylan whispered, gripping her hand to his heart.

"I found your mom. I hid her and some children behind a curtain. I couldn't get them all, Zy. I tried. Amity found your brother, his wife, and their children. They're being protected in Therian territory," Neri whispered back, feeling the relief flood his body. "Amity called on Bane and his people to help. She woke me out of a deep sleep to warn the others."

"And my father?"

Neri paused. "Well, this is a little awkward."

"Was he killed?"

"Yes and no. The Order didn't kill him. But yes, he's dead. I shot him, in the heart. I knew it was a kill shot, and I took it. He attacked your mother as she held children in her arms, all because she wouldn't leave them behind. Then he came at me. I warned him, Zy, but he grabbed me. I won't ever be abused, *never*. I don't care who it is. I'll kill them," Neri said, drawing a line in the sand.

Zylan pulled her under his arm. "I'd have killed him too. Anyone who touches you or my mother or anyone I care for... I'll end them."

"Let's go find your family and go home," Neri said, both of them walking away from his old life, toward their new one.

So many innocents had fallen under the darkness of that night. So many had given their lives—and for what? For Strain and his hate? Not good enough. Neri knew Des would have her hands wrapped around Garm's neck soon enough, learning everything they'd need to know about how to kick Strain's ass back into the hole he'd crawled out of.

Chapter Twenty

Strain had spent an hour trying to put a word to the feeling that was eating him up inside. The only word that came close to it was failure.

Failure, a noun—an act or instance of failing or proving unsuccessful. Failure, in any other definition, was the act of not performing to the expectations of the Genesys. It was going against his word, thinking you somehow knew better than someone who has walked the earth longer than sin had tempted man.

Failure had a flavor all of its own. It filled his mouth with the taste of curdled milk and rotting meat. It twisted Strain's stomach into a powerless knot, one that only grew with each gulp. It filled his nose with a stench he couldn't quite describe—rank and sour, like an unwashed carcass that had been sitting in the sun or found on the side of the road, served up as Strain's last meal.

Strain stood with his head held high in the back room of his sound studio, waiting for his father. There would be no running from him. His father was everywhere and nowhere. He was a fucking ghost. Worse than that, he was the darkness that made shadows that lived in every corner and crack.

Strain had expected a report on his desk by mid-afternoon, or, at the very least, for Garm to stroll through the door with his cocky smile. *Mission completed, again*. When there was no report and no Garm, he went looking. The Order had not returned. Neither had his little puppets. No one had returned.

Strain had tried to make his way to Sola-Nosfer, but

had never made it there. The grounds were crawling with Therians. At first, he thought the wolves had come to scavenge, until he saw the Slayers walking with them, communicating with them. From the back hills, he watched more Therians, the wereleopards and werebears. They were all banding together. The irregulars were forming alliances right before his eyes. Groups who had killed each other were now working together toward one common goal. His attempt to wipe out Sola-Nosfer had created a union between groups.

He'd failed at a task that had been planned right down to the smallest detail. It had still been disastrous. He'd gone over every detail in his head. It should have gone perfectly. It should have happened exactly as planned.

"You can't run from fate," the Genesys spoke, his voice rolling out from all four corners of the room. "You did not plan for everything, Strain. You did not plan for your own pride and self-admiration. You did not plan on your own fate. You did not plan for the blinding hate you hold for your brother."

Through gritted teeth, the voice of the Genesys felt like pins were being driven into his brain. Strain snapped. "Cael. Is. *Not*. My. Brother."

The Genesys took form in front of him. Strain didn't need to see his father's face to see that he was smiling, and it wasn't the kind of smile you'd have plastered on your face when running into a long lost friend. It was the same smile Strain had when he was about to pump a bullet into a friend's head.

"You stand as an equal? Surely you do not see yourself as my equal?" His father's words crippled him, bringing him to his knees. "I've asked you a question."

"No, I do not see myself as an equal," Strain replied, his words whispered out in a stranglehold.

"I didn't think you were that foolish, although your foolishness is a constant surprise." The Genesys paced in front of Strain, who was on his knees, as he usually met his father. "You say Cael is not your brother. You have claimed many times that there is no love lost there. For there to be a hate this thick, there has to be love. There is always a balance. With darkness, comes light. With cold, comes heat. With the moon, there is a sun. With hate, there is love."

Strain shook his head. "Once I loved him. Once. That love is no more."

"Ahh, so there is only blinding hate. This hate has caused yet another failure, another loss."

"I will rebuild," Strain spoke more for himself than his father. He'd told himself that very same thing the moment he'd walked away from Sola-Nosfer.

"In your own words, *'You take from me, I take from you.'*"

Strain lifted his head, tilting it with cluelessness.

"Indeed, son of mine. Everything of yours is already mine." The words of the Genesys felt like blistering hot slices down Strain's psyche. "You hold on to these human values and weaknesses. You hold on to hate and a greed for victory. Again, human values. Yet you fail, time and time again. You are blind, and this blindness blocks your path every step of the way. You love and hate. You starve for the destruction of a group that demolishes everything you have built. Your focus is on Cael and his Slayers, but you forget that the bigger picture is not about them."

"I will not make this mistake again, Father," Strain whispered, head down, feeling defeated.

"I am certain of that, for you will have no abilities to use, to create the world you have in your mind. Do you think I cannot see what your wishes are? Do you think I cannot see your plans for my death—for you to take over and rule? You forget about balance. You forget about rules and agreements. You lie to save your skin, only to fall back into your human ways. Since you enjoy these human ways so greatly, they will be my gift to you."

Strain's body twitched, then pitched off the floor. He stretched his mouth into a scream that would be eaten by the darkness of the Genesys.

His father leaned into his face, grinning, as the darkness swallowed Strain's head. "What is it you always say? Ahh, yes. You can't run from fate."

The Genesys repeated the words Strain had said for months, whispering them into his mouth as he pulled Strain apart from the inside, sucking away the darkness inside Strain, back into his mouth. Then the Genesys pulled his mouth away. Strain couldn't feel his limbs. He couldn't feel his own eyes blinking. He was in complete darkness.

"You will remain here, with me, for one month. And in that one month, the irregulars will take everything from you. You will start anew. You will rebuild without abilities. You will rebuild as I see fit, or your next punishment will be death."

Strain heard nothing more. He didn't know if he was standing or on his back. He felt nothing but pain and a crushing emptiness.

He was afraid, but not even the word 'fear' could cover what he felt inside. Where his humanity had once lived was nothing more than a void of darkness. Anything that formerly resembled who he'd been, what he'd been, who he'd killed to become, was gone. His identity was removed and replaced with bone-crushing terror. The shell of a man he'd once been was left dangling in the darkness of his father.

Part of him wanted out. He had to get out. It was the kind of darkness that light couldn't penetrate. Yet, to be released was to go back to nothing. Everything was gone, taken from him. He would be nothing.

The darkness had come, as he'd known it would. But he was the only one to have been taken by it. The darkness had eaten him and everything he called his. The darkness had chewed him up and spat out the bones, keeping everything valuable. He tried to close his eyes, but he could feel nothing. It was just as dark either way.

Chapter Twenty-One

Locked and loaded, they were ready. Every Slayer was on deck, armed to the teeth and jumping out of their skin to take down the Order. Garm, who was still being held captive at the compound — soon to be turned over to Sola-Nosfer for tryhal — was interrogated by Des.

"I'll never talk," Garm spat in her face.

Des stifled a laugh. They were always big and tough until she got hold of them. *If he only knew.* Everyone else in the compound knew exactly what a touch from her could do to a man, and they were scared shitless. She would either eat their memories or give them ones that made burning to death feel like minor sunburn.

She pulled up a stool and removed her gloves. "I don't need you to say a word. In fact, your silence will be a big help."

Des didn't run her hands over him, as she'd learned. She grabbed onto his arms. She was in for the brain kicking of her life, but she held on. With Zylan, Sid and Riam at her back, she'd endured hours of this. Finally, getting everything she could possibly get from the piece of shit, she was done. Then Sid carried her out of the room. He tucked Des into bed, beside her Aegys, her Fyrvor, where she could sleep an entire day away. He'd eagerly waited for her there. Des rarely used her abilities to the extent that she'd needed to for Garm with Cael in the room. His need to protect her broke her concentration.

She'd seen more than her heart could handle. Broken, she clung to her mate and let her sadness wash over and out of her. Cael, her man of worth, stood guard, holding her, soothing her, making love to her. As she faded into sleep, she knew he'd do whatever it took to show her life and love and remind her what the hell they were all dying for.

* * * *

Captain Salas Warner, Captain for Team One of the Netherworld Taskforce—the monster squadron—leaned over the long wooden table at the compound. Maps lined the table from one end to the next. When he spoke, everyone listened. He didn't waste words. He didn't use small talk, and he demanded attention. If he thought someone had something better to do than paying attention to him, he'd knock them on their ass as a reminder of what was more important. This was life and death. He didn't have time for bullshit on his taskforce. He'd boot anyone who didn't take it as seriously as the father who'd died to protect his family or the mother who'd fought off a Hellyon to save her children.

This was all or nothing. No member of Warner's team wanted to be the idiot who made the wrong choice. The task force, once seen as a joke, was now the place to be. To be kicked off Warner's team would land them at some desk job or punching out parking violations on Blood Alley, either of which would make a person eat their gun.

"We're cleaning house tonight, boys," Warner spoke, giving Des a wink. She was never insulted to be considered one of the boys. "A citywide curfew is in effect. Tonight there will be no tryhal. We are judge, jury and executioner. No one gets a hall pass. We have been given the green light for a complete cleansing of the poison running in our streets. We are taking out any trace of the Rancor Order. No one stops until the threat of the very fucking sun sends you into the shadows. But in those fuckin' shadows, you fight. You fight until we have scoured the filth from our homes. You fight until you fucking die. I will accept nothing less. Those who give up, do not come back. That failure will earn you a bullet with me standing over you, ripping the dog tags from your neck. You will *not* have earned the honor of those tags."

Warner marked the maps with the information that Des had dragged out of Garm. Little dots decorated them. These were where the Order stored either chemical or Proletaryans. They would hit every hideout and cache of weapons, drugs and men. They were taking them down, hitting them with everything they had. Everyone connected to the Rancor Order would be taken down, fast and hard.

"Keep tight. I want to go home and hug my wife and children. And I want to be able to look my wife in the eyes and tell her that our children have a fighting chance," Warner spoke, eyeballing each man and woman in the room. "I want to see each and every one of you back here at dawn. Team, drop your letters on the table and muster."

Each of Warner's men stepped forward, placing a letter to their loved ones on the table. If one of them didn't make it back, their letter would be delivered to the address on the front. No one wanted to have to deliver it, but Warner wouldn't hit the streets without each letter accounted for. He was a hard ass, but Zylan and everyone else in the room respected the hell out of him.

"This isn't for complete strangers. You're doing this for your family. You fight to get your asses back for them," Warner said, pointing to the table. "Move out."

"Hooah!" the room sounded off in unison. Warner's words had been heard, understood and acknowledged.

Zylan turned to the sound of Neri and Ester talking. Neri was dressed in full gear and carrying medical supplies. Seeing her dressed for war made him hard, yet it scared the shit out of him.

"Let's not do this again, Zy. I'm coming, and that's final," Neri said, shaking her head, not bothering to wait for his objection.

When she'd found out about the skirmish, she'd started packing supplies. Zylan had tried to reason with her then dropped to his knees and begged her. When that had failed, he'd panicked. He'd gone through a cycle of grief, right down to the anger and final acceptance.

Zylan nodded and swallowed the bile trying to crawl its way out of his mouth in the form of a gut-wrenching scream. He pulled Neri to the side of the room, touching her face, only now realizing the torture Cael went through every time Des went out on a hunt.

"I love you. Please, dear Orygin, be careful out there," Zylan whispered, his fingertips shaking against her cheek. "I'll die without you. I won't make it, Neri, unless I have you."

Neri lifted to her tiptoes, kissing his nose. "I love you. We will meet up here at dawn. Don't be late."

He smiled, nibbled on her bottom lip then said, "I'm never late."

Bane cleared his throat, grabbing their attention. "Sorry, guys, but, Neri, we have to go. My people are waiting."

Neri and Ester would be escorted by a small pack of Therians for protection. Bane was in charge of Neri's team. He would be in full shift. Zylan trusted Bane to have his back any time, but this was different. This was more than his life. This was everything. Neri wouldn't heal like Zylan would. She couldn't take a bullet and shake it off. She was like the finest piece of china teetering on a ledge during an earthquake.

Zylan gave Bane another hard look. "Bane, please…"

Bane clapped Zylan on the shoulder, giving it an understanding squeeze. Bane stepped in front of Zylan and went down on one knee. "I am a wolf who does not stray from its path. With the very last breath in my body, I will see she does not stray from hers. I will protect her with the lives of my people, unto my death. She shall be my moon. I will follow her to the edges of the earth."

Bane's words calmed Zylan. He knew Bane would die before leaving Neri without protection. Zylan wished he could be the one to watch over her, but also knew he would be the one to get her killed. His concentration would be lost. He would fight in fear. She would pay for it. It was the same reason Cael and Des were hugging in the other corner. They would not fight together either. Zylan gave Neri one last kiss then watched her run from the room, Bane at her six.

"Let your faith be bigger than your fear," Sid said, as he moved up to Zylan's side. "*Love bears all things, believes all things, hopes all things, endures all things. Love never ends.*"

"Corinthians. I honestly didn't think you had ever read the Bible, much less could quote it," Zylan said, jabbing Sid in the ribs and laughing.

Sid smiled, rubbing the back of his neck. "First time I've actually quoted scripture, but I thought you needed it. I'm not saying she's not coming home. What I'm saying is that she doesn't have to be here for you to love her. You will always have that love. No one can take that away from your soul. Your soul never forgets."

Sid stepped away, leaving Zylan wondering what had made the Watchyr get so sappy. Zylan let it go, focusing on his thoughts of his Fyrvor. Zylan would see her again, either way—in this life or the next. He would pray to the Orygin that he could hold Neri's living body in his arms again. If they were fated to be together, they would be. They would both fight tooth and nail to make it home on time. It was all they could do. Zylan would use that love every step of the way tonight. He filled his heart with hope and faith then pushed forward. He would need it each time he kicked down a door.

* * * *

Neri crawled through the rubble, Bane crawling behind her in full shift. Her hands were bloodied. Some of it belonged to her and some from the dead and dying. She remembered stories from her *haraboji*, her grandfather. He'd fought in the Korean War and had suffered greatly.

He had said the true measure of a man was not in how great he could kill, but in how brave he could be in the face of death. Bravery had nothing to do with your fear.

More than that, it took courage to crawl through bodies to get to your people. It took courage to drag your own bloodied body to those who were too brave to scream out for help. Their silent bravery kept her alive. Neri would honor them by pushing forward, taking on her own injuries.

Bane bit at her boot, stopping her forward movement. She didn't make a sound. He wouldn't have stopped her without reason.

To her right, what was left of a brick wall hid her location. She could hear the shuffling in the debris. Straining her ears, she could hear whispers. They were heading in the direction of where she knew a man was trapped under rubble.

She looked back to Bane and held up two fingers. Bane nodded his head awkwardly. He could hear them better than she could. He could hear each individual's heart beating. She slowly let go of her medic bag. Her gun had been in her hand since the very first explosion. They had lost two Therians, an hour ago. It was just her and Bane. Closing her eyes, she calmed her body. Years of meditation would be of use now. She grounded herself.

She opened her ears to every noise, right down to the settling dust. She breathed in the air, smelling blood, wolf and rotting. She felt the ground under her—the rocks and glass, bits of wet flesh and the coolness of old blood. She focused on the two men moving toward her downed man.

Bane pulled on her boot again, trying to give her a look. He didn't want her to do this. She knew it. She gave him a look back. She was doing it with or without him. Bane let go of her boot. He'd be in this fight if she was.

She lifted her hand and motioned three fingers. He nodded his large and furry head. One finger, two fingers... She closed her eyes and lifted the third finger. In one solid movement, she stood and fired her gun twice, hitting both.

Bane was over the wall and on them, bones snapping, screams muffled under the pressure of his jaws. One final snap and they were both down, gone from this life of evil cruelty.

Neri grabbed her bag and ran. Her ears were still in tune for sounds she should worry about. She stepped over bodies and on top of them. She wanted to show respect for the dead, but she was out in the open, and she couldn't avoid stepping on a few fallen, here and there.

Her breathing coming hard and fast, she didn't remember holding it. She focused on the task at hand. The man on the ground was a civilian. She'd thought he was one of Warner's, but it was just a man, clinging to his metal lunch box. His wedding ring glinted in the moonlight that was now shining down inside the broken building.

"I didn't scream," he whispered. "I knew you would come. I saw you."

Neri lifted her finger to her lips. She needed him to keep quiet. She didn't know who else was out there, or who might be listening for little whispers. She scanned his body, and her breath caught in her throat. The rubble that had trapped him was also the only thing keeping him alive. The edge of the cement beam that had come down on top of him was lying on top of his chest, and it was what kept him from bleeding out.

Bane growled, the noise vibrating deep into her bones. Neri didn't have time to react. The trapped man's lunch box clanged against the rubble, as Bane pushed her down onto her side. The gunfire echoed in her ears, bouncing off the broken walls and metal.

She could hear bones snapping and flesh tearing. Turning over, she saw the trapped man bleeding out from a shot to the chest. She scrambled in the broken bricks, cutting her knees and hands. Pulling herself to his chest, she pressed on the new wound.

He pulled his ring from his finger and pried Neri's hands from his chest. "Mable, her name is Mable Wright."

158

"Hold on, please," Neri whispered, her eyes filling with tears, but he was gone.

She grabbed the ring and pushed it into her vest, cursing under her breath. Bane pulled at her with his teeth. It was time to move on. She knew she had to, but she was angry — so bloody angry.

"He was just going home from work," Neri whispered. "Going home to his wife. He was a civilian. He had nothing to do with this — nothing."

Bane growled again and pulled at her, whining. She knew she had to get up. She knew she had go to. She was forced to leave this man who'd just saved her life behind, like something less than a precious soul. He was more than garbage, more than useless, but she left him. She picked up her bag and followed Bane down Blood Alley. She followed him to the next wounded man — and the next.

Neri had her gun out and ready. She didn't wait. She fired for the man who wouldn't make it home to Mable. There was no mercy left inside her. She recited the Hippocratic Oath, the first version she had learned, the classical version her mother had framed on her office wall, a gift from her father. Her mother had lived by that oath every day of her life. And when her father had passed, her mother recited that oath. It reminded her of her mate.

"I swear by Apollo Physician and Asclepius and Hygieia and Panaceia and all the gods and goddesses, making them my witnesses, that I will fulfill according to my ability and judgment this oath and this covenant," she repeated. Neri moved from body to body, doing what she could and taking a moment of silence when she was too late.

She found Ester hiding out. Her Therians were long gone. They pushed on, reciting the oath together. Hearing Ester's voice had calmed Neri, keeping her focused.

"Do you think we breached the oath? I mean, I just stabbed a guy in the throat with a knife I pulled out of his vic," Ester asked, grinning.

"I don't think that applies. I'm sure there's a loophole or

two. I shot a guy in the eye. I'd thought he was a good guy. I patched him up, he pulled a gun and I shot him. I mean, I spent ten minutes on that fucker, only to kill him. Waste of my damn time," Neri replied, finally laughing. She knew it was the stress taking over, but she did find it funny.

Bane led the way. Ester would treat them, and Neri would stand guard. She took out anything that Bane growled at. At each location, she prayed she wouldn't find Zylan. She made Ester call out from the bodies if it was Zylan. Neri needed the reassurance. She was going nuts, thinking she'd stumble on the body of her Fyrvor. She knew that if she'd found him, she might as well die out there beside him. Without him, it wasn't a life. She'd merely exist in a world that meant nothing.

Finally, with an hour until sunrise, Bane whined. When she felt a hand on her shoulder, Neri didn't register that it could be a good guy. She grabbed the arm and pulled the body forward as she leaned. She pulled with everything she had, yanking him over and onto the ground in front of her. Still holding his arm, she spun, locking the wrist and pressing a blade into the throat of the man who'd touched her.

Bane sneezed, resembling what Neri thought could be a laugh.

"I'll take that as a no, you don't want to walk home with me?" Zylan asked, grinning, holding on to her wrist.

Neri closed her eyes, looked up to the sky and shook with gratitude. Her chest vibrated with silent sobs. "Orygin, thank you."

Zylan pulled her down to his chest and hugged her bloodied body. He was clearly just as thankful. "Let's go home, Fyrvor. The fight is over. The wounded are being packed out."

Walking hand in hand, Neri and Zylan met the rest of the Slayers on Blood Alley. Looking around, tonight Blood Alley had truly earned its name. The good guys had suffered a great many causalities. The Slayers had lost four new recruits. Bane's people had lost a dozen, trying to protect Ester, Neri and the Slayers. Warner's men would be grieving eight deaths. Almost fifty civilians, all caught in the middle on their way home from work, had perished. The men and women who weren't able to afford a night off had paid with their lives, while trying to put food on their tables.

Countless injured were being reported. Every Slayer needed stitches and bandages. Once home, Ester and Neri refused to remain in the compound. They followed Bane into the woods, to honor his people. They'd given their lives for Neri and Ester to make it out alive, and they would honor the fallen Therians and their sacrifice for a war that had only touched their homes when they had been asked for help. They paid tribute then left Therian territory, leaving them to their grief and customs.

Zylan had waited for Neri. She found him leaning against the wall in the den, safe from the sun. They went back to their room. Together they washed the night from each other. Delicately they loved each other. Dried, they wrapped up in bed — safe, alive and stronger than ever.

The darkness had come, and it had fought a good fight, but the Slayers had fought harder, hand in hand with the Netherworld. They'd fought with love and with faith, and they'd fought for those who couldn't fight for themselves. They fought for goodness, for a future they all prayed for. They fought for hope. Their inner light was bright enough to wash the darkness away. In its wake, the darkness had left broken walls, blood-soaked streets and torn families. Strain may have knocked them down, but they'd gotten back up, stronger than before.

"I love you, Fyrvor," Zylan whispered. With Neri tucked under his arm, he lifted her hand and slid his mother's ring onto her finger. "Marry me. Do me the honor of being my wife. I promise, I'll never be late."

"Yes," Neri whispered back.

She let herself crack wide open and cry in his arms. She

was thankful, genuinely thankful. They'd made it back, together—a blessing so many were not granted on this night.

Once she'd thought she'd be single for all time, with no room for someone in her world. Then she'd found Zylan. She'd found someone who would sit at her feet while she worked for twenty hours straight. He never complained about the hours she put in. He would bring her food and coffee, sharpen her pencils and would re-braid her hair. He would sit happily with her talking about things he didn't understand, but he would enjoy every word. He would research with her, pulling up information on the computer, and he would read the reports to her.

And when Zylan would return from his hunts and she was asleep at her desk, he would make sure everything was saved and backed up, put everything away exactly where it belonged and carry her to bed.

Zylan had never once pressured her into consummating their relationship or pushed her for anything more than a kiss and his arms around her as she slept. He never questioned it. He never mentioned it. He let her heal, and he was there to talk to when she woke up from nightmares. Zylan had started doing yoga with her, grunting and snapping, then he would tackle her to the floor with a kiss or tickles.

He was Zy, not a Prince, not a Slayer. To her, he was just...Zy.

He was the man who loved her more than life.

Chapter Twenty-Two

One month later

Zylan and Neri helped Sola-Nosfer rebuild, with the aid of the Therians, who would assist with guards until the Vampyres could restore their ranks. A treaty was struck between the Vampyres and the Therians. The Vampyres paid tribute to the Therians for their sacrifice. Therian territory, once taken by the King of Sola-Nosfer centuries ago, was restored, with interest. It was a start, and both sides were willing to build on it.

Zylan took the crown, only to step down and give it to his mother, Queen Zylamon-Vhenom Bloodletting. She would rule, as she should, over a new dawn for her people. She, unlike Zylan, knew what changes needed to be made, in order for their people to flourish. She knew of the abuses that had occurred against the women of Sola-Nosfer. Those who did not agree would be banished from their lands.

Zylan was proud of his mother's actions. Her first order had been to abolish the traditions of forced marriage and the Vestal Virgyns. Those who wished to remain could do so of their own free will, but this would never again be by force. Their training would no longer include how to accept abuse. In fact, they would be trained in self-defense. They would be schooled in subjects that would help their community, not just their mate. Vestal Virgyns would be given options to go to school, to earn degrees, to learn of the world. They would never again be shut in, like caged animals. They were no longer seen as objects. They were beings. They had souls, and they would receive the same honor as everyone else.

The queen's second order of business had been that any act of violence or degradation inflicted upon another being would be seen as an act against the throne, against the queen herself, and punishable by death. There would be no tolerance for suffering. And anyone who witnessed it and did nothing would carry the same blame.

The queen had made these announcements with Zylan and the rest of her children at her side, the Therians behind them. His mother had held a hammer with a hammerhead almost as large as her own head. With a swing, she'd smashed a hole into the side of the tomb. Zylan had had no idea that she was so strong. The tomb was to come down, and the pieces used to tile a fountain, in memory of each Vestal Virgyn who had been entombed. Sola-Nosfer would never again entomb a member of their society. These acts that the queen had referred to as barbaric would never again be allowed within their city. His mother had also formed a special sisterhood, led by Amity, whose job was to seek out those in the world who'd suffered. The suffering would be offered sanctuary within the walls of Sola-Nosfer. Zylan couldn't think of a better person to head up this new sisterhood than Amity.

Zylan was most pleased that according to his mother's mandate, those who were still alive from the council who had fled during the battle, leaving the rest behind, were removed from council rule. They had taken oaths upon taking their seats. They'd sworn that they would faithfully execute all that the king commanded, that they would never desert Sola-Nosfer or its people and that they would not seek to avoid death. Instead, they'd run and had left the women and children to fend for themselves.

Zylan and Neri had stood and watched the tryhal of Garm, for his acts against Sola-Nosfer, then the acts against the mate of their Prince. Neri had tried to have that charge removed, but the queen would not hear of it. Any act, such as the acts ravaged upon her body or any other body, would be met with death. Garm hadn't begged for his life until he'd stood on deck with a noose around his neck. It was there that he'd tried to bargain. He would give them Strain. But he'd not been spared. He was hanged in the town square for all to see. Zylan was proud that his mother would show no mercy to anyone who came against the crown or against those she loved. The point was well made.

His mother the queen, once seen as a meek victim, had a voice, and you'd be damned to ignore it. No one grieved the king. He'd been a bastard, and everyone knew it. A small funeral was held within the queen's chambers. Although he was a bastard, the queen still held it. Because to her, he still deserved this honor, for he gave her children. For that reason alone, she honored his ugly soul.

* * * *

"I think I'm going to be sick. Please don't let me puke on the queen," Neri grumbled, pressing the palm of her hand into her chest. She looked out of the small window. The grounds of Sola-Nosfer were crawling with Therians, guarding her special day, her wedding day. All but one were there. Only Bane was inside. She wouldn't let him miss this day, not after all he'd done. The Slayers were her honored guests, as were the Therians.

Zander smiled as he watched her pace back and forth. "If it makes you feel any better, I passed out. I was overheating, nervous and collapsed. I cracked my face on the stairs and broke my nose. We got married with gauze shoved up each of my nostrils. Thankfully, we were in Vegas, and it didn't matter. Our wedding pictures show Evil holding me up, blood dripping down my face."

Neri laughed, picturing it in her mind. "You didn't get married here?"

"Oh hell no. We went to Vegas. Zy was footing the bill. We lived it up and blew twenty grand on the slots."

"I bet he was thrilled."

Zander shrugged, a small smile slowly forming. "He didn't care, really. He wanted us to do what we wanted to do and screw the rest. He's always been that way with me and my sisters. Whatever makes us happy. He wanted us to do it, and he'd suffer the wrath of my father."

Neri stepped forward, touching his hand. "I'm sorry about your father."

Zander laughed. "Don't be. On my tenth birthday, my mother allowed me to have a small party. Man, I was so excited—my first real party. She was beaten in the town square until she could no longer stand. I didn't know it was happening. I was partying it up with my friends, while my mother was almost killed for that party. I hated him."

Sid poked his head into the back room, dressed in a suit. "Ready to rock, Doc?"

Neri gave a nod. "How do I look?"

Neri stood in the same wedding gown her mother had worn, her *hanbok*, sheer white top and deep purple dress, with gold accents at the waist and wrists, with a long gold ribbon down the back. Her hair was pulled up in a tight twist with little purple flowers on the side. Her feet poked out to show her deep purple slippers.

Sid stepped into the room with one of the kinder smiles she'd seen him sport. He lifted her hands and placed a kiss in each palm.

"You're breathtaking, straight from the bosom of Elysium, touched by the Orygin and blessed by each Watchyr. Zylan will swim in your beauty for all time and be nourished by your love for him," Sid whispered into her palms. He looked up with a wink. "In other words, Doc, you're hot as fuck. My man Zy is going to shit his pants when he sees you."

Neri grinned, rolling her eyes. "Sid, you say the most beautiful things."

Sid revealed his usual lecherous grin then placed her hand on Zander's arm. "I do my best."

Sid stepped into the hall that was laced with the finest of

white silks. Letting out a small whistle, he cued the music.

"Thank you, Zander, for doing this for me." Neri felt her eyes tingle.

"I am honored to walk you down the aisle. Your father would have been here if he could have, but I tell ya, he's watching you now, and I know he's proud."

Sid poked his head back into the room. "Come on, already. It's an open bar. Open fucking bar. Remember what I said. Run down the aisle, toss your flowers at some single chick, scream yes, grab the pen then sign your name. I'll meet you at the bar with shooters. Ten minutes, tops."

With a smile and a deep breath, Zander led her out and into the hall of the banquet room. The room was filled with people, hundreds looking at her. The walls were covered in white silks, small twinkling lights and thousands of candles hanging from the ceiling. Soft music carried her from the back of the room to Zylan. At the front stood the queen and to her left stood Amity, who didn't try to hide her happiness. With an ear-to-ear smile and eyes glittering with tears, Amity gave Neri an approving nod.

* * * *

Zylan watched his future walk toward him. She radiated beauty and promise. Once her eyes had found his, he watched the calmness flow into her shoulders, and she raised her chin a few inches. A soft smile formed on her face and melted his heart. He lifted his hand and pointed at his watch.

He mouthed. "Come on. You're almost late."

She gave him a playful look, running her hands down her body. She whispered, knowing he would hear her, "Shut it. This shit takes time, asshole."

She failed to realize the entire room would hear her words. Small giggles carried over the music. Zylan laughed. He took in every detail of her, which only added to her beauty. The closer she got to him, the more rubbery his legs felt.

"I'll catch you," Neri whispered, stepping up to his side. Zander placed her hand in Zylan's.

The moment they touched, he was rock-solid steady. They both turned to Zylan's mother. Her face was pure happiness. She no longer governed her emotions. If she wanted to cry, she did. If she wanted to laugh, you could hear her for miles. She dabbed her eyes and gave them both an approving nod.

The ceremony lasted almost an hour, most of it a blur to Zylan. He kept zoning out on Neri, both of them lost in each other. Every few minutes they'd each receive a nudge, bringing them back to the ceremony.

Finally, it was over. Amity stepped from the front, smiling, holding a white silk ribbon to bind the new lovers together. Zylan's right hand was bound to Neri's left. The queen used a small blade and dragged it across the unbound hands, their blood dropping onto the white silk. With blood, they were bound.

"Come here, beautiful," Zylan drawled, pulling Neri into his body, kissing her harder than ever before.

The room erupted with clapping. But before Zylan could drag Neri off, Neri paused. Zander came to the front with a small white box. Neri knelt in front of the queen, lifting the box with her one free hand.

"Please accept this token, a show of the children to come," Neri spoke with a shaking voice.

The queen lifted Neri to her feet, her eyes watering. "Never kneel at my feet again. You are a being, not an object of lesser value."

The queen opened the box, smiling. Zylan was lost as to why she would smile at a box of dates and chestnuts. Zander leaned in, filling him in on Neri and her Korean wedding traditions—how the bride offered these to the groom's parents as symbols of children. The parents then threw them at the bride, who tried to catch them in her wedding dress.

Neri stepped back, taking her mate with her, still bound

at the wrist. She lifted one side of her dress and Zylan grabbed the other, smiling. The queen threw the dates and chestnuts, laughing and smiling. They caught three.

He would never forget the smile on his mother's face or the laughter of his mate. Moving through the room, he couldn't hear anyone else, only her laughter. He saw nothing but her face.

Through the reception, he was in a daze. They laughed. They sang. They danced. They ate. They drank, and they would love. Carrying her from the banquet hall, he kissed her with every step he took. Into the bedroom they shared at Sola-Nosfer, he placed her on the bed. He moved through the candlelit room, bringing back her favorite night clothes and turning his back, still smiling.

"This is the happiest day of my life," Zylan spoke, telling her how much he loved her and how he would honor her.

"I'm ready," Neri called out, as she usually did once she'd changed.

Zylan turned, still grinning, and froze. His jaw dropped wide open, and his eyes were threatening to roll from his head. Neri wasn't in her night clothes. She was in the middle of the bed in a small white lace bra and panties, stockings landing mid-thigh. She'd pulled her hair down, letting it fall in waves around her shoulders. The grin on her face staggered him.

Zylan grabbed onto one of the posts of the bed, staring.

Neri got up and crawled toward him on her hands and knees. When she got to him, she climbed up the front of his body, pulling his face to hers.

"Please, Neri, wait," Zylan whispered, his throat dry and instantly hoarse. "Are you sure? I mean… We don't have to do this. I am content with never doing this. I never have to touch you that way."

"Come here already." Neri giggled. "I want you, husband. Now."

Zylan swallowed hard, taking in a deep breath. He

staggered again, clutching the post. "I think I'm going to pass out."

Neri started to laugh until she saw his eyes roll into the back of his head. His feet went from under him, but instead of going backward, he came forward, like a sack of potatoes. His forehead smashed into Neri's nose. A loud crack echoed throughout the room. Zylan was on the floor, and Neri was on her back, blood pouring from her nose.

Rolling off the bed, she yelled for help. She knew Bane would be close. He was always close. Bane swung the door open, gun drawn, with the rest of the Slayers behind him.

"Where are they?" Bane screamed, scanning the room, looking for the bad guys. The rest of the Slayers fanned out, yelling for whoever was in the room to come out.

Cael ran to Neri's side, lifting her up. "Who did this to you?"

Zylan was laughing on the floor, "Oh my God. Zander is going to love this."

Neri started to laugh. "Zy passed out. He landed on my face."

Zander's laughter could've been heard all the way to the city center. He staggered into the room, holding a bottle of champagne, laughing until he made no sound.

"I love it. I so fucking love it." Zander cackled. "Sorry, Neri, but this is absolutely hilarious."

Ester, drunk as a skunk, was still damn good at triage. Thankfully, Neri's nose wasn't broken, just bruised. The room emptied, leaving Neri and Zylan alone again.

"How about you lie down. I'll clean up. I don't think you should be standing when I come out." Neri laughed.

Zylan grabbed her hand. "Neri, you're hurt. Why don't we wait?"

Neri knelt in front of him, lifting his head. "What's this about, Zy? Do you not want to make love? I wouldn't force you. You can say no to me. I love you and support you if you're not feeling comfortable with this."

Zylan let out a shaky breath. "I don't want to hurt you.

I'm scared. I'm scared to do something that'll make you feel like you're back in the bad place. I don't want you to hate me. I don't want to hate myself. I don't want you to leave me. The list is long, Neri. But most of all, I don't want to ruin this or how you feel with me."

Neri lifted up, kissing his lips. "You would never hurt me, Zy. It may be uncomfortable at first, but that has nothing to do with hurt. Be there with me, completely, and there will never be a bad place. Make love to me. Give me new memories. Give me pleasure, and it will never be ruined."

"Swear to me, right now, that you'll tell me to stop when you want me to stop. Swear you will do that, or I can't."

Neri stood, kissing his forehead. "I swear to you, but I know you. You would stop the moment you thought I needed to. You know me, Zy, just like I know you. Now, strip and wait—but not on your feet. I think you'd rip my nose completely off next time."

Her laughter filled the room as she walked away. He did as she had asked. His clothes were on the floor, his shirt destroyed from trying to get it off before unbuttoning it. He waited.

He'd never been this nervous before. When he heard the water turn off, he was glad to be sitting down. Fumbling, he turned on the iPod and speaker system that sat on the table beside the bed, flooding the room with soft classical music. The sound was enough to keep him from crawling out of his skin.

"Are you ready?" Neri called from the bathroom, sticking her leg out of the door, showing from foot to thigh.

"Yes... Yes, I'm ready," Zylan whispered, trying to speak up.

Neri poked her head out of the door and winked. She stepped out in a little black sheer nightgown that hung just over her rear. Her little black lace panties covered less than tooth floss would have covered.

She moved up the foot of the bed, yanking the covers off

him. He placed his hands over his groin, instinctively. She kissed up his legs to his thighs and pulled at his hands. Reluctantly, he let his hands fall to the side. Even soft, he knew he was large.

"Wow." Neri blushed.

Zylan tried to cover himself again.

She grinned and pushed his hands away. "Challenge accepted."

Zylan flinched when Neri's mouth closed around him. She licked from base to head. He closed his eyes and gripped the sheets in his fists. It was unbelievable, the pleasure he felt from her in a split second.

With him growing in her mouth, she pushed her head down for one more long stroke. He knew that once he grew to full length, she'd never be able to deep throat him. She came up and slowly worked him with her mouth and hand.

"Wait. I won't last. Wait, please," Zylan stuttered, pulling her up by the shoulder.

Neri climbed onto his hips, kissing his mouth. "We have tonight and tomorrow and the next day and the next. It doesn't matter, Zy."

"Please." Zylan moaned into her mouth. "My turn?"

Neri giggled, nodding. He lifted her with one arm, twisting her around and setting her onto the bed. He knelt between her legs and pulled her down by her ankles onto her back. Slowly, he hooked his thumbs under her panties, keeping his eyes on hers. She chewed her lower lip, nodding again and lifting her hips to help him.

He tossed them onto the floor in the middle of the scattered buttons from his ripped shirt, and he sighed. She opened her legs more, exposing her exquisiteness to him. She was perfect, so unbelievably perfect.

He lifted each leg, kissing her toes and feet, making her giggle and squirm. He kissed up each leg, flicking his tongue on the backs of her knees. He honored her body. He worshiped her, as any good mate should.

Helping her sit up, he gently lifted her nightgown over her

head. Her ivory skin lit up in the candlelight. Her breasts were small, yet voluptuous. They shone in the flickering light of the candles. Her little pink nipples were tight and hard, making his mouth water.

Neri arched her back, inviting his mouth. Holding the back of her neck, he tilted her head back. Placing small kisses on her face and jaw, he neglected no part of her body, as his mouth made its way to her rosebud nipples. He took one in his mouth, and the sigh she released reassured him to continue.

He pulled her hips toward him, laying her down again. His mouth stayed on her breasts, exploring every millimeter, as his hand massaged her hips. Her groans and the rocking of her hips told him to continue, to bring her the pleasure her body needed, to bring her the release her body craved. He could smell her need, almost taste it on the back of his tongue.

Slowly, he moved his hand to her thigh, to find her stretching her legs open farther, inviting him to her core. Touching her had rocked his world. It was like being caught between a fire and ice. He needed to taste her. He needed to drink down that pleasure and fill his belly with her.

As if she could read his mind, she pushed at his shoulders. "Zy, please, please."

Zylan dragged his kisses down her ribs to her hips and beyond. He dragged his tongue between her lips. Her wetness covered his tongue, drenching him in her scent. He breathed her in, the smell firing in his brain, sending shock waves into his cock. He almost lost it. Pressing himself into the bed, he focused on Neri.

He sucked her clit into his mouth, flicking the tip with this tongue. He slid first one finger into her wetness then two, preparing her for his size. Flicking faster and curling his fingers over her G-spot, he had her bucking against his face. She held his head against her.

With one long scream, her orgasm racked her body. He held her hips down, forcing her to ride it out. Not giving up on the sweet spot inside her, he massaged her until the waves of her intense orgasm subsided.

Zylan climbed up her body, watching her face. As she settled, he withdrew his fingers. He couldn't stop himself. He cleaned off his fingers with his tongue. He couldn't allow himself to waste a single drop of her pleasure.

"More," she groaned, sitting up and pushing him to his back.

She climbed onto his hips, pulling his upper body to meet hers. Kissing him and tasting her own orgasm on his lips, she lowered her body onto him. She growled into his mouth, taking his entire length into her, inch by inch.

Zylan moaned as she rocked on his hips. He thought of only her and her pleasure, not of his own. She leaned back, slowly bouncing on his hips. The sight of her sent his brain into fits. He grabbed onto her and rocked with her. Lifting one hand to between her legs, he furiously rubbed at her clit.

Fisting the sheets, she screamed. "Now!"

As her orgasm slammed into her, his broke loose, and, like a starved animal, it ate. He came with so much force that he couldn't breathe. He couldn't think, and he couldn't move. Neri ground her hips over him until he was a pool of liquid satisfaction.

Pulsing inside her, he pulled her down onto his chest. Her ear pressed to his pounding heart.

"Is it too soon to ask for more?" Neri giggled into his chest.

And that's all it took to start rounds two and three—and four. Round five came after a shower and dinner. They had spent the day locked away in the bedroom, dancing to classical music, feeding each other berries and whipped cream, taking a bubble bath and strengthening their bond. Nothing, not even death, would break it.

Chapter Twenty-Three

Like any storm that crashes down, the darkness eventually fades. But the damages left behind can be insurmountable. One month served in darkness, a punishment that Strain would always remember. It was crippling, like any storm would be. It would cement Strain's hatred for the very blood that had given him life.

Released back into the world—one that would kick his ass—he cursed his father. His men—or what was left of them—were scared shitless and wouldn't come out of hiding. He couldn't control his puppets, the only two remaining from the raid. He had no choice but to put them down. Every cache had been seized by the Slayers and the Netherworld Agents. Every compound and safe house was leveled. All assets and property were snatched by the Netherworld. Everything that was linked to the Rancor Order had been destroyed.

When he read about the citywide raid, Strain's revulsion had only grown. All his father's punishment had done was create a chasm for him to fill with seething hate. There was nothing left of who he'd been, his accomplishments or his work. But he would rebuild. He would learn from his mistakes and not make the same ones twice. He may have been down, but he sure as shit wasn't out.

He didn't care if he ended up spending years in that hellhole of pitch blackness. If he destroyed Cael, it would be worth it. Any punishment his father dished out would be worth it too.

He still had The Hemlock. The papers weren't public yet. From there, he'd make a new army, in his image. From his new digs, he'd slowly run Blood Alley and rebuild the Rancor Order — stronger, deadlier and crueler than ever before. There would be no forgiveness, not from him. The shred of humanity that he'd held on to, he'd left back in the darkness. His father's punishment had created a human without a soul, like the rest of the men who found their way down Blood Alley.

Deagon Jackston was back and would be front and center. Strain was gone, left to wither in the hellhole with his father. He had two targets — Cael, his brother, and the Genesys, his father.

He closed the door behind him in his new office at The Hemlock, his 'Plan B'. The Slayers had taken almost everything, like Strain's father had. But he always had a backup plan. He wasn't stupid enough to put his own money on the line with the Order. That's one thing his father had taught him — always have a 'get out of jail free' card.

Time with his brother had taught him how to fight and survive with nothing. He could also thank his father for that. It was him, after all, that had dumped him on the streets as a baby. He'd learned straight from the womb how to make it in a world that couldn't give a fuck about you or your pathetic problems. There was always someone else with bigger problems and a shittier life.

A soft rap at the door brought his attention from his hate.

Prudence leaned in, her hair pulled into a high, tight bun. She was all business. "Deagon, the girls are ready for the night. Garm still hasn't shown up for me to go over the rules. I've hired someone else. Sorry. I know you wanted your friend to be involved, but I can't leave my girls unattended."

Deagon. He liked the sound of his name. "I agree."

He looked down the list that was on his desk, names of the ladies of his night. He stopped at one name in particular. "Send Des in."

It was short for Destiny, but he'd call her Des, for tonight at least. And as she proved her worth, bending over his desk, he screamed out her name... Des' name. As he pounded every inch of himself into her juicy little cunt, he hated her. She represented everything he hated about himself. Each of them fucked the other. The only difference between his hate for her and her hate for him was that she made a few bucks off it.

Strain realized, as he zipped up his pants and kicked the whore out of his office, even Deagon was a cock-sucking, hateful sinner of a man. Deep down, Deagon was worse than Strain. Perhaps it was Strain who was the sham, and Deagon was the mastermind who egged Strain on.

You could dress it up and call it whatever made you walk taller, but a bastard was still a bastard, no matter what mask he wore that day.

Chapter Twenty-Four

"Mable Wright?" Neri asked, as a woman pulled open a large oak door.

Mable looked like she was in her late forties, until she stood in the sunlight. The sun kissed her skin in a way that removed the ages. It added youth to her eyes, which were puffy from many nights of tears. The lines in her face showed years of laughter and joy. Each line, Neri knew, was worn with pride. She could only hope to wear the same as her own badge one day. In the background of the house, the sounds of tiny feet and laughter filled the halls, mixing with Neri's favorite classical music station.

"Yes?" she replied, straightening her pink and yellow apron.

Neri tried not to cry as she thought of the day Mable had been told of her husband. She had probably opened the door in the same way, with her kids running in the background, only to be told that life as she knew it was over. Every hope she and her husband had was gone. Every dream they'd shared would never come true. They would never hold each other again.

"I knew your husband for the briefest of moments. During the raids, he saved my life but paid with his own. He gave this to me." Neri reached into her pocket and pulled out the wedding ring.

Mable breathed out, letting out a small laugh that sounded more painful than humorous. "That was my Walter, a good man, even in his last moments."

Neri placed the ring in her hand. "I have no words that will take away the pain that saving my life has brought to you and your family. Please know that you are in my prayers every single night."

Neri stepped off of the front porch and down the front walk.

"Miss, you left your briefcase," Mable called after Neri, who didn't turn around.

Inside the case, Mable would find Neri's entire life savings, the deed to her house and the business card of a lawyer who would give her the paperwork she'd need. It was enough money to give her and her children a good start at the life they'd been robbed of. Neri could never repay the sacrifice, but she would give everything she had to a family that Neri had learned had nothing. They were on the verge of eviction and had needed the money more than Neri ever could.

* * * *

"I'm proud of you," Zylan had whispered, when Neri had crawled into bed with him after her visit with Mable.

"I'll never be late," Zylan said as he pulled her hips into his. He ran his fingers down her side and right to her swollen button. She was always wet for him, always ready to take him into her body.

She turned her head to the side, pulling his head to her throat. His lips curled back and he fed from his Fyrvor. He was home—finally, home. You can't run from fate. He couldn't believe he'd tried.

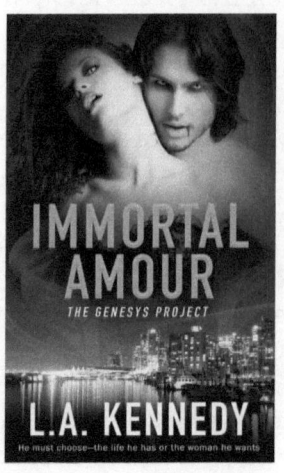

Immortal Amour

Excerpt

Chapter One

Midnight crime scenes... Of all of the crime scenes to be at, Des favored these ones.

Darkness had this way of stealing the truth. Des was thankful for that, as she stared down at the ruined remains of what she thought had been a man. There was so little left. It could have been just about anything, including an animal carcass. She was pretty sure a small cow hadn't been tossed off the beaten path, which left only one thing. The broadness of the shoulders, or what was left of them, told her it was a man—was, the key word. It once was a man. In the pitch blackness of the summer night, the blood took on a different color altogether. Black liquid tar pooled under the bloated remains.

Desdemona Bloodworth—Des, to those who knew her—had worked her fair share of cases for The Netherworld, policing the little slice of in between, where life and death, man and monster, were as subjective as ivory and eggshell. Born a Kler'voient, a Prophetyc, she was born with a second sight. To her chagrin, her sight was limited to the past. They called it a gift, a rare and valuable talent, so she'd been told. She called it what it was — a burden and a curse.

Her curse, like a coin, had two sides — one side for good and one side for evil. Should she choose the wicked and shiny side of the coin, Des could control thoughts, giving someone memories that made them jump off a bridge or into the path of an oncoming train. Alas, she chose the good side, the dull and virtuous. And there was nothing nearly as fun with the side that landed on morality. On this side, she was the one that was left with the memories and the desire to toss herself in front of a train.

Des was the end result of what had happened when an angel and demon crossed the unspoken line, creating what the Orygin had forbidden. She was good and evil, yet neither, with the ability of both. With a soul that sits in Pergetore, she tried to earn the feathers on her wings to pull her soul out of there. So far, not so good, case in point, she's still fucking here.

A deal struck between the Orygin and Ruynous said that the winged couldn't be locked away in Hades and half-breeds could not walk the earth in full power. Each good deed earned a feather for a set of wings only Des' soul could see and feel. A full set would force the Wardyn to expel her soul and she'd be home free. Until then, Des and her soul were stuck in a perpetual rerun of a shitty reality TV show called life.

The Netherworld had been in existence since mankind had become perverted, spitting out beasts and burden. An irregular gene had been activated by the Genesys, the creator of the Rancor Order, for an absolute unquestioning army. He'd tried to play God and screwed them all. Anyone who had been born with this dormant irregular gene had become something more and less than man. Cue the reason the Netherworld had come into existence.

The Netherworld was similar to any other police task force, roping in those who broke the law. Only this flavor of criminal had fangs and claws. Fangs and claws were what Des hated the most. Pesky little things they were. The locals called in the twisted and perverted her to help catch the twisted and perverted them. It was the circle of life around here. Des wasn't one to complain, much. It paid the bills and for the therapy that she should be going to.

She worked some of the most gruesome cases due to her 'gift'. Most people were rotated off the grisly and heinous crimes every few years, human or not, or they washed out and crawled into a bottle. She was burned out and had already been in and out of a bottle or two.

But here she was, at midnight, leaning over the remains of a body, bloodied and left for the birds and critters, trying to earn another feather for a set of wings she couldn't see.

The body lay on its side. Claw marks ran down the back and front of him, like a hot knife through butter. The pale white skin, drained of blood, had been sliced and gouged, ripped from the bones and laid over him like a safety blanket. Innards had been spilled onto the gravel, still shiny in the moonlight, reflecting the stars and flashing police lights. It was almost beautiful, the still calmness only death can bring, had it not been for the whole 'dead and torn up' part.

The second body lay roughly ten feet away. Des' eyes focused on the lumpiness of his remains, like a sack of red, broken potatoes. *It's odd how your mind will focus on trivial facts*, she thought, noting the oddities that came to mind, like how dirty the intestines were or how the hair wasn't messy enough. For a moment, she wondered where he had his nails done. Her brain tried to pull away from the horror with thoughts that didn't matter, thoughts that kept the truth of what she was looking at, at bay. It was an irritating fail-safe when she was on the job and the job was dealing in horror.

The second body had been ripped open, his chest splayed and insides removed completely, leaving him an empty sack of what once was a person. Des had stared at him, not a drop of blood had touched his perfect face, but the horror of the night was etched deep within it. She wouldn't forget the look frozen in his glossy eyes and slackened jaw.

In daylight or utter darkness, some things couldn't be lied about. Fear was fear. It didn't matter how much light shined down. Fear didn't care what kind of spotlight it was under. Fear was like Mother Nature. It didn't think twice about wishes or timing. It just was. It had its own timeline, its own needs, and it didn't give a shit about anyone else's. Fear didn't discriminate. It didn't hate or care. Fear was fear for all. Fear hung in the air, coating skin like jelled sweat—like the remains of Mother Nature's fury.

The bodies were lost under the canopies of the trees. Des rubbed the goosebumps from her arms, grateful that she didn't have to stand beside them—smelling them, seeing them and mourning their deaths. From yards away, she could disassociate, divorce her emotions from the heinousness of the night. From here, each could be an 'it'. She could lie to herself at a distance. From here, they could be bodies and nothing more.

For now, anyway…

About the Author

L.A. Kennedy

L.A. Kennedy, beyond the story…

L.A. Kennedy is a Canadian born writer, living in the ever-growing city of Vancouver, Canada. Here, she spends her days getting lost in the beauty of reading and writing. L.A. Kennedy mainly writes fictional books. And can be found researching myth, folklore, and everything in between, with a special interest in edge-of-your-seat paranormal romance. L.A. Kennedy can be found behind a mountain of books, on any given Sunday.

L.A. Kennedy's writing credits include two hit series that mix mystery, horror, paranormal romance, fantasy, and intrigue.

L.A. Kennedy loves to hear from readers. You can find contact information, website details and an author profile page at https://www.totallybound.com/

Home of Erotic Romance